ORANGE SKY & BLUE SUN

Subhadip Mazumdar

Invincible Publishers

First published in India in 2019

ISBN : 978-93-88333-40-5

Invincible Publishers

201, SAS Tower, Sector 38, Gurgaon-122003

Registered Address: Opposite Kasturba Ashram,
Radaur, Haryana–135133

Printed in India by Excel Printers Pvt. Ltd.

To my Beautiful wife and Best Friend Sarmistha. I would not have been able to make this attempt without your support and belief in me. Thank you for teaching me how to find happiness in simplicity.

Acknowledgement

I would like to thank the people of Kolkata where I lived and grew up. I would like to thank all the people who I had interacted and worked with during my creative days of theatre in Mumbai. I thank my parents and my teachers. Finally I would like to thank my readers for their support and who inspire me to live my life as a Story Teller.

Contents

We Have All Changed

The night sky appeared like a beautiful dusky woman decorated with gold ornaments. Ashima rested her head on the edge of the window. She could recognize the city that she was returning to after a decade as her flight made its descent, dropping through the layers of the cloud. She was feeling excited and eager to reach the city where she grew up, eager to meet her parents but as the plane touched down, she began to feel uneasy. She thought for a moment, if there could be a way the flight could take off again and disappear into the cloud of darkness.

She stood in the queue to go through the immigration, when an immigration officer who was controlling the crowd of passengers, noticed the Australian Passport in her hand.

"This is for Indian Nationals, please use the other queue for foreign passport holders," he said pointing to a shorter queue adjacent to where she was standing.

She had garnered an unnecessary attention since the time she had stepped out of the aircraft, walking towards the immigration, and waiting for her luggage to arrive, next to the conveyer belt. She had observed curious looks among men, women, staff, passengers, and especially the middle-aged bald bespectacled immigration officer who could not stop staring at her, even after he had stamped and returned her passport. It seemed quite difficult for the people in the city that had lit up to usher Goddess Durga home, to accept a woman as tall as her, little more than six feet on a flat heel.

The warm but festive Kolkata air greeted her as the sliding doors opened for her to push her trolley out of the terminal. There was a sea of people outside, some holding name tags and others keeping a keen vigil to spot their dear ones. She spotted Bharat-da[1] among the crowd; her father had mentioned in an earlier phone conversation that Bharat-da would come to receive her.

Bharat-da had become part of their family, he had been employed as a driver when she was a kid. Her family had Mark IV Ambassador then. He looked much older to his age now, which Ashima quickly calculated in her mind to be no more than fifty-five. She had waved a few times at him. He had not even bothered to look at her and seemed to continue his search in the crowd of passengers coming out of the doors which opened and closed on its own. She reached up to him, managing to push her way through the crowd, and tapped him on the shoulder.

"Bharat da, let's go. You did not recognize me."

---

1 Bengali word to address elder brother

He turned to look at her in total dismay. He took over from Ashima to push the trolley to the open car park of the airport, where their Toyota Corolla was parked.

Ashima tried to recognize the city, as their car came out of the parking lot and joined the VIP Road that headed towards Ballygunge. She could not recognize much of the city that she had left behind a decade back. It was well past ten in the evening and she could see most of the shops closing down. Many more bars and pubs had opened up on that street. Women were flocking up in groups on the street in front of most bars, trying to make a trade. A new clock tower had come up on a stretch of road, it was probably Kolkata's answer to London.

Life size posters of politicians covered walls all around the streets of the city, as were the hoardings of the new Bengali films that were to be released in that festive season. Although it was another three weeks before celebrations for Durga Puja[2] to begin, the city was well decked up. The bamboo structures that resembled the various wonders of the world and housed the idols of Goddess Durga were going through the finishing touches. The city was almost ready for their biggest annual carnival.

Her parents, Sumita and Ashish, were sitting around the dining table in the left side of the staircase on the ground floor of their house. The dining table was laid with Bengali culinary delights featuring basmati rice, bhetki fish

---

2 Biggest religious festivals for Bengali community

fry, lentils, fish and mutton curry along with sweet tomato chutney. Sumita had instructed the lady that cooked for the household to prepare all of Ashima's favourite dishes. At sixty-five, she could not take the strain of standing for hours to cook by herself. She had supervised everything that was cooked that day seated on a chair that Karuna, their full time servant, had brought into their spacious kitchen. Ashish who had turned seventy recently, rose slowly from his chair as he heard the car stop at their driveway. He turned towards Sumita in anticipation as he tried to suppress his excitement.

"Come, come quick!" Sumita shouted, sitting at the dining table as she heard footsteps climbing the short flight of stairs towards the main entrance.

"Ashim…" she said as she entered the dining room.

"Ma" she said almost in continuation, making it sound 'Ashima' in union.

They looked at her in anticipation of the return of their prodigal son. They had forgotten his fight to become her, as Ashima touched the feet of her parents in quick succession. They were happy to have their child among them.

Ashima had always fought and detested the Ashim in her since the time she could feel him. She remembered as a five-year-old, destroying couple of her mother's lipsticks trying to imitate her. Her mother had laughed at him then, she would even dress her as a girl and he looked quite pretty. Her father, who was a well-known lawyer in Kolkata, then Calcutta, had always resented his mother, dressing him as her. He had always wanted Ashim to be the alpha patriarch just like him, his father and grand-father. They were all lawyers and he had assumed that his son would be one too. Ashish was very proud when Ashima was born as Ashim, that he had maintained the family tradition of having a son and had already begun planning on how he would pamper his grand-son.

Sumita saw Ashima sitting on a chair in the balcony that faced the main road next morning. It was 6:30 a.m. but the morning sun was already bright and radiant on the eastern sky. She saw the layered hair that ran past her shoulder with the golden streaks on them from behind as she walked towards her. They were hanging by the backdrop of her pink satin night dress. Sumita wondered if her son's heart had now been beating as a woman. She walked up to Ashima and kept her hands on her shoulder. She wanted to cry in complain and ask the million questions that she had for her mother. She was her mother, a woman, yet why she had not understood his pain, his fight and flight to become her. Ashima looked at her mother and the woman in the mother understood the questions in her eyes.

"Are you happy?" Sumita asked.

"Yes, and liberated," the daughter replied as Karuna brought in the tea. He seemed to wear a confused look as he had seen photographs of a baby, who was a boy, turned adolescent and then a man on several walls of that house, so who is this woman now.

The mother and her daughter sipped the tea. “Shall we go shopping later today, Gariahat?” Sumita asked.

“Chinese for lunch after shopping,” she replied with a smile and then continued.

“Ma, can I borrow your bottle green sari with golden borders. I remember you wearing it in a few of my birthdays.”

Sumita nodded her head in consent as she got up slowly from her chair, feeling the pain in the joints of her knees from arthritis that she had been ailing from a while now.

“Has Baba come to terms with his daughter now?”Ashima questioned with a smile.

“Give him some more time.” Sumita said while leaving the balcony. She could not see the pain hidden in her daughter’s smile.

Ashima observed a group of sparrows that had perched at the far side on the long railing which covered the length of the balcony. She had wanted to get up and go to her room, but decided to laze around and watch the chirping sparrows. They appeared like a bunch of adolescent school kids enjoying themselves before the morning assembly, oblivious of how the day would unfold, and the challenges that it could perhaps throw at them. The sparrows reminded her of Ashim Ray and his adolescent friends in the missionary school.

Ashim was different from the other boys in his class. The difference became more distinct during his adolescence years. He always wanted to escape things most boys would like to do like playing soccer especially when it rained, playing hand-cricket before the morning assembly, and curiosity in girls—waiting at the bus stand after school hours to catch a glimpse of the girls from the neighbouring girl's school.

Much to the dislike of his friends, he was more obedient and attentive in class. They made fun of him when he performed dance forms that were practiced more by girls than boys in the talent contests. He was as good at dancing as he was in studies. He never understood and felt like them. He was a favourite of the female teachers who taught them, especially Bengali, English, and History. He related more with them and their challenges when the boys in his class would misbehave with him. They ridiculed him, called him names, one in particular, that he remembered was Brihannalla[3].

Ashim detested the feeling that it was indeed a man's world. He disliked how his father had sometimes crushed

---

3 Name assumed by Arjuna in Hindu epic Mahabharata for a year when he a disguised as a woman. It also lightly referred to a transgender.

the feelings of his mother. Sometimes, he even wept in silence, and cried aloud naked in the shower as the sound of the water silenced her anguish in his body. Looking at his own naked body in the mirror in his room, he felt captivated by the growing femininity within him. He had felt it even more after finishing his tenth standard, when he turned sixteen. There was something sweet about it that appealed to him. He was a handsome man for the world, tall, fair, slim, and had been a source of attention in most social gatherings. Once, a very beautiful girl had proposed him at an inter-school music festival. He had felt quite surprised about it.

On the other hand, he always had a fancy for Chanchal, his classmate. He was among the few that spoke nicely with him, never making fun of him. He liked him as a man. It was a time in his life when hormones would overrule rationale, and he would not even care about natural and unnatural to the way the world had defined the acts. It was during a lunch break in their school, Chanchal had kept his hand on Ashim's sitting on a bench in the school garden. He let it be. Chanchal had in a spur of the moment caught his hand and walked out briskly from the garden. He had felt like a woman being swept over by her man. He consumed the 'her' in him, locking themselves in a toilet on the second floor.

Her thoughts were interrupted when Sumita returned to tell her that breakfast was ready, it was her favourite, loochi[4] and cholar dal[5]. The sparrows took their flight.

She looked beautiful as she descended down the staircase in a bottle green sari with golden borders. The bottle green airhostess blouse appeared slightly loose as they hanged around her arms. She wore gold earrings that her mother had kept over the saree in a jewellery box on her bed. She had taken her time to dress herself to perfection in the same room, looking at the same mirror that had held her captive for so many years.

Sumita smiled at her daughter and called out to her husband, “See how beautiful your daughter is looking. I feel like putting a black dot on the side of her forehead to protect her from evil stares.”

Ashish was busy turning pages of the morning newspaper sipping his second cup of tea of that morning in the dining room. He lifted his head slightly, gazed over the rim of his reading glasses and smiled in acknowledgement. He saw the happiness on Sumita’s face. Ashima looked very similar to Sumita when she was younger. Sumita looked back at her husband with a smile, but failed to recognize his emotions.

Has he come to terms with his son’s transformation to be his daughter now? Is it more from a view of the

4 Indian bread typical in Bengali household

5 Chick pea lentils

questions that he would need to answer the society when asked, that made him angry? Did he ever try to understand his son? He had lived his life with authority and success but seemed to be in a battle of denial with himself for a while. The thoughts crossed Ashish's mind as he gazed at the newspaper not caring to read a word in there. He had held it in front of him to escape the world around him.

Ashish had not resisted when Ashim wanted to go to Australia for his post graduation after his graduating in Economics from a reputed University in Kolkata. Sumita did not want Ashim to go, but her husband convinced her. He had told her that it would make him more of a man, and to allow him to live by himself for a while. The truth in his mind was different. He wanted his son to be out of his sight, away from the society he lived in.

It was two years ago that his son had transformed to become his daughter. Ashim became Ashima through a Sex Reassignment Surgery. She, then he, had prepared for it over the last two years. He felt liberated as she. Ashish and Sumita had last seen their son two years ago in Canberra, where Ashim taught Economics. He had even refused for his mother to come to visit him at the time of his surgery. They were numb when Ashim had informed them about his plans and the process over dinner during their visit to Canberra. They had not told the world about their daughter yet. They were both awake in silence that cold July night in the bed.

The mother and her daughter enjoyed their time shopping, navigating through the crowd as it built up through the late morning. Ashima bought a lot of things, artificial jewellery, ethnic attires for herself, sarees for her mother, Punjabi[6] kurta and dhoti for her father, and souvenirs for her friends back in Canberra. She felt happy and accepted. She had walked through the same footpaths with shops on both sides, navigating the crowd before too as Ashim, but never with the same exuberance of Ashima. Sumita observed the happiness in her daughter, like a bird that was caged for long and now set free, soaring the sky, with her wings spread out. They even had Chinese food in her favourite restaurant located in one of the narrow lanes along the Gariahat Market. She recognized the faces of some of the waiters who had since aged, they could not recognize her.

Couple of days went by in the Ray household. The servants had now had their inquisitiveness answered; they got a view of the past from Bharat da and understood the present. Sumita had grown closer to her daughter than she was ever with her son. She had seen her pictures and had video calls, but never before this trip had she held her daughter's hand. She had asked the Lord in silence why did she not give birth to her as a daughter. The communication of silence however continued between the father and his daughter.

---

6 Indian Ethnic wear

It was a couple of nights before Ashima was scheduled to fly back to Canberra, and about ten days before the start of Durga Puja celebrations. Ashima heard the sounds of sitar floating from their drawing room. She could recognize the raga being played. It was her father's favourite. As a child she had quietly seen him play, and even as an adult once or twice a week. She imagined while seated in front of the mirror in her bedroom upstairs, that her father was playing his sitar seated on the rug on one side of their huge drawing room. He would often do so when he felt happy, occasionally sipping into the single malt from an expensive cut glass, between each raga that he would skilfully play on his sitar.

She wanted to see her father play again. She rose, stepped down the staircase and entered the drawing room quietly. Her father was playing a raga with his eyes closed, his fingers moved over the strings in utmost dexterity. She waited for him to finish and then clapped. Ashish smiled as he looked at his daughter, seated on a chair right in front of him.

"You play very well Baba," she said and then continued after a pause, "do you feel embarrassed because of me?"

Ashish was not ready for this question. She had also not planned to ask the same, but somehow it flowed out of her heart. It was an honest question, perhaps little too honest. She also was probably little tired of interpreting his silence and needed an answer.

"No," he said as he placed his sitar carefully on the rug beside him.

"I am proud of what you have done, it takes courage to listen to one's heart." His eyes moistened as he spoke. She sat down next her father and looked into his eyes.

"We have all changed," her father said, unable to stop the tears from rolling down. He felt very happy in that moment. He seemed to have won his fight of several years with himself.

Ashima stayed back as the Ray's celebrated Durga Puja together. It was the best they had ever celebrated. Ashish was able to kill the Mohishashur[7] in him, their Durga had truly come home that year.

---

7 Demon

Time To Go

"Time to go inside, Didimoni[8]." Pronoti said as she walked up slowly next to the wooden cot in the veranda, on which Didimoni lay. The winter sun was setting in the horizon far away from where Didimoni lay. The December dusk had set in earlier than usual, much to the annoyance of Didimoni. It meant that she had to return to the confines of her room much earlier. Pronoti helped her sit and quickly covered her with a blanket. Didimoni took considerable time to sit up and a little bit longer to get down from the cot. She slowly walked into her room, supported by Pronoti, the door of which was adjacent to where her cot was placed.

A dim candescent bulb barely lit up the large room which was occupied by two large wooden beds. They were old and heavy. The wooden beds were artistically carved and had a small mirror attached. Didimoni's husband, Rudra Narayan Sanyal had got them made by carpenters with a lineage of making beds for the royals. They were almost seventy-five years old. She looked at the curves on the wooden bed with pride as she sat slowly on one of the beds, assisted by Pronoti.

8 Elder sister addressed with utmost respect

An antic dressing table separated the two wooden beds. She looked at the empty bed in front of her. It was occupied for most part by her elder daughter, Sudha. Sudha passed away two years back, she was seventy-five then and was exactly sixteen years younger to Didimoni. The bed had no occupant after her demise. Didimoni had always asked Maya to sleep on that bed at night. Maya was the night attendant for Didimoni and was more comfortable sleeping on the floor. She would be with Didimoni from seven in the evening and give her company, feed her dinner, tell her stories of the village. Didimoni used to wait eagerly all through the day for her arrival. She had in fact forced her grand-sons to ensure that Maya was offered dinner every day.

Everyone called her Didimoni. She was not sure how it all started. She could not even remember when was it the last time someone called her by her name, Dakshayani Debi. At the age of ninety-three she had outlived her three daughters. She also bore a son just after Sudha, but he could not survive beyond ten months in this world. She would often complain that she had long over-stayed her tenure in this world. She would ask the almighty at every evening prayer of her in the Sanyal household, coinciding with the sounds of the conch-shell[9] and the rattles of the bell, when her time would come to depart. She had seen more than she needed, daughters, grand-sons, grand-

9 Ritual in many Bengali households to blow conch shell in the evening for household bliss and usher positivity.

daughters, great grand-sons, great grand-daughters, even her great grand-daughters were married now.

"What more do I need to see?" she would ask Pronoti every evening while she combed Didimoni's hair. "You have to bless the great great grand-children as well," Pronoti would repeat every evening. She was Didimoni's grand daughter-in-law. Her daughter had also been married.

"Will you take me outside the house tomorrow? I want to see the roads outside the house. So many things must have changed," she requested Pronoti.

"We will see. Your hair is done, see how pretty you are looking now, have to run to organize dinner." Pronoti got down from the bed slowly as she kept the comb on the dressing table on her way out.

"Hasn't it been more than ten years since I have gone beyond the wooden cot on the veranda," she said.

No one heard her, Pronoti had already left the room by then.

"What time is it?" she asked, hoping for an answer, instead there were crickets and some frogs that responded. She looked through the door and felt the chill. Maya walked in to the dimly lit room. The bulb flickered as the voltage fluctuated, which was very common in a small town on the borders of Bangladesh.

"Is it seven?" Didimoni inquired again.

"Seven-thirty, I am little late" Maya answered as she tied the mosquito net to the four wooden stands that were attached against the corners of the bed.

Didimoni slowly laid down on her bed, Maya helped her and then tucked the mosquito net around the sides of the mattress.

"Rest for a while, I will get your dinner after some time."

Didimoni lay captive on her bed, surrounded by the mosquito net. She heard the voices of her grand-sons. They had returned from work. They were now busy in conversations with their wives and kids. Not all her grand-children lived in the house, only two of the five lived there, rest had moved to Kolkata for greener pasture.

Most of the rooms in the palatial house remained locked as did also the Gods in the temple. It was her father-in-law who had built the house and the temple at the entrance of the house. It now stood neglected—a far reminiscence to its former glory.

The age of outsourcing had not even spared the Gods. The temple was outsourced to a priest who offered prayers once a day in the morning. The priest was given a monthly budget to execute a minimum scope of services. He ensured that it worked profitably for him, even though the Gods stayed hungry. Didimoni thought that she was at least better off than the Gods in the temple.

Didimoni was back on her wooden cot the next morning. She sat there like a queen, carefully monitoring the activities of the busy morning. The long open veranda that formed a large square, with a courtyard in the middle was busy. There were rooms across its periphery opening onto the veranda as it made its bends. The ones that were not locked had continuous requests shouted out from them. The men shouting at the women to serve them their breakfast. The women shouting at the maids to check if the rice was boiled to perfection, and to strain the starch quickly. The great grand-children negotiating for some additional pocket money. She saw everything but could not remember most of the names that were part of another busy morning except for Pronoti's. It was not uncommon at her age and she had accepted it. She was only worried that she could not remember the face of her husband clearly and even more that morning. There was an anxiety and an excitement within her that she could not understand. She felt like the young girl that she had been many decades ago, who had put on her best clothes and about to step out of her home to visit the village fair.

She saw Payel, her great grand-daughter going past her wooden cot. She asked her softly to help her wear the red saree that was carefully stored in the trunk below her bed. Payal seemed to be in a hurry and besides, felt best to avoid the responsibility. She stopped beside her momentarily and then yelled to her mother, Pronoti, and successfully passed on the responsibility.

Didimoni made no further request, she slowly tried to lay down on the wooden cot in the veranda. She realized that she could not do that without assistance. Shyama, another grand daughter-in-law of her, saw her struggling, as she was coming out of her room that opened onto the veranda. She quickly came to Didimoni's assistance. She left after covering her well with her blanket.

The morning sun appeared bright and warm on the winter sky. It provided her with warmth and comfort, as its rays fell on her to provide some company. She felt better. The activities in the household had now quietened. The men and the younger lot had left to attend their respective responsibilities. Didimoni gazed around, her eyes searching for something or someone. Her search stopped at the corner of a tall cylindrical pillar on the veranda to her right. The veranda had more than dozens of them all around, supporting the roof, above which ran the expansive terrace. She lay looking at one corner of the pillar. It appeared like a face, a formation created by paint that had scrapped off and stains formed over and around it.

She knew the face but struggled to recognize it. She smiled at it as she heard a voice that addressed her as Bou[10]. She had heard that voice before and there was only one person that had ever addressed her with that name.

---

10 Wife in Bengali

She struggled hard till she finally recognized the face on the pillar. It was her husband, and she felt the warmth of her tears overwhelming her dry eyes. She met his eyes with a shy smile as Dakshayani would, as a young bride.

"Yes," she said under her breath. She had never addressed her husband by his name. She had always responded in yes or no, and mostly started a conversation with, "Listen or are you listening?" Her mother had told her at the time of her marriage that it was not auspicious for Hindu women to address their husbands by their name. She had thus never uttered her husband's name aloud.

Didimoni saw young Dakshayani following the tall frame of young Rudra Narayan during the ritual of their Saptapadi[11]. The Hindu Brahmin priest had tied the end of her red Benarasi saree with the end of Rudra Narayan's shawl. She had followed him seven times over, around the sacred fire. She did not understand much of the seven vows that the priest had chanted during each of the seven times they went around the fire. She only knew she had to live with him in a new home, sharing a room in a house full of strangers. During the ritual, Rudra Narayan had carefully looked back at her over his shoulder, with each step they had taken together to complete their vows around the sacred fire. He would check if she was keeping up with his pace and would some time even slow down his pace for his Bou to catch up. She knew from then that she could follow him blindfolded for the rest of her life.

11 A ritual in Bengali weddings

Dakshayani was welcomed with lots of love and warmth by her in laws. The entire house was lit up as she entered the main entrance, dressed in a bright red Benarasi saree, covered with jewellery, but what she was most proud of were the red and white bangles that she wore. She wore vermillion in the middle parting of her hair and a big red dot on her fair forehead. She looked like a queen next to her king. Rudra Narayan wore a white silk kurta with gold embroidery all round in floral patterns and white cotton dhoti. He looked every bit a king as he greeted guests with a smile that made his thick black moustache spread wider over his lips. They made a couple none could miss and the entire village had queued up for a glance.

Didimoni saw a young woman dressed as a bride, wearing her bright red Benarasi saree and jewellery all over, walking slowly towards her from the other end of the courtyard along the open veranda. She could not see her face very clearly but noticed that people in the household were walking past the young bride without acknowledging her presence. She could see her face clearly now as she stood by her next to her cot. She looked up at her adjusting her head on the pillow.

"Sorry, I got a bit late in bringing your breakfast today." Pronoti spoke loudly while walking towards Didimoni from the other corner of the square open veranda, where the kitchen was located. She did not notice the beautiful young bride who stood by her wooden cot. She had pulled up the edge of her saree to cover her head just enough to show the part of her hair, which was anointed with red vermillion. She also wore a red dot on her forehead, red and white bangles. She watched Pronoti as she sat next to Didimoni.

"I am fed up every morning managing this chaos, I am tired of this. I also need rest. I am also getting old." Pronoti continued without any response from Didimoni.

"Come here let me help you get up. I had soaked the chapattis in warm milk for a while now, it will melt in your mouth, and you will not have a reason to complain." She kept the large bronze bowl next to the pillow. She yelled in disbelief when she touched the cold body of Didimoni. She was staring at the pillar, her eyes wide open, a smile locked at the corner of her lips.

"Come let's go Bou, what are you waiting for?" said the tall man, dressed like a groom to the young lady standing by the cot where Didimoni now lay, dead. She did not respond and was looking at the people who had gathered around the cot. They were crying.

"Time to Go, Bou," the man said as he lent his hand forward for his Bou to hold. They walked through the veranda, towards the door that opened into a passage to the main entrance, passing the temple on their right.

Daskhayani looked around one last time before stepping outside the main entrance of the house, through which she had once walked in as a bride many years ago.

Didimoni finally saw the road outside her house.

Shombu Salesman

The candle flickered one last time with all its brightness, before darkness filled the room. Shombu stared at the darkness till he escaped all mortal pains. He had fought hard and seen his dreams. He even saw most of them butchered as he had tried to fuel them with hope, each day with more. It was hope that kept him going till he ran out of it. He was not literate, but became educated with the ways of the world by the walking the streets of life.

It was a busy summer morning. Bandel[12] station was bustling with most passengers trying to board overcrowded trains to Howrah station to reach their offices in Kolkata. Shombu, then a twenty-one-year-old promising rat poison salesman had jumped into one of the compartments on a Howrah bound train. A slender man with a dark complexion, he had learnt how to navigate his way through the crowd inside the train since the age of thirteen. He wore a chocolate colour trouser and a bottle green half shirt, one of the two he had. He did not heed much to the abuses and annoyance of the passengers as he glided himself through them, pushing them around to

12 Bandel is a small town, located in the state of West Bengal, India, about 40 kms from Howrah station.

reach the central passage, his workspace. He only smiled back at each abusive face.

His father, who was also a salesman in those same trains, had told him often as a sermon and trade secret, "Develop a thick skin, never react always smile." His father was a successful salesman and sold combs of various sizes, before he died a tragic death. He fell off from a running train and was severed. There were tears in the household for a week and a bit, and then life took on with its flow. Hunger and survival won over grief and despair of losing a dear one.

On reaching his workspace, Shombu started his craft. He was eloquent in his sales pitch. He defined the problem statements, articulated the key pain points that the rats caused to households, particularly to the housewives, menacing their lives from messing up the kitchen to tearing clothes, and thus, neglected husbands.

"The only saviour from all these troubles that will restore conjugal bliss was Jibon branded rat poison," Shombu shouted. Jibon, which in Bengali meant life, was indeed a matter of getting life back for the responsible husbands in the compartment by buying the Jibon brand rat poison.

Shombu sold well, he offered bulk discounts, remembered to collect credit from some passengers, as well offer implementation advice. "Mix with whole wheat dough, they like it," he advised a passenger. He would even ask consultative questions on the colour of the rat, to their sizes, before pushing an extra packet or two to a customer. Shombu was a star, and built great stakeholder relationships. The passengers missed him on the days they did not see him on the train. Shombu would say, "Oh, yesterday I took the up train the other way, not towards Howrah. But Howrah passengers are much better. That side, they do not understand the effect of Jibon rat poison on their lives."

It was just after Shombu's twenty-fifth birthday, on the insistence of his mother, that he got married to Shanti. Shombu was hesitant initially, but it was only after Togorbala, his mother, threatened to leave him and spend the rest of her mortal days in Benaras[13], that Shombu agreed on the proposal.

Shanti was petite and vivacious. She had just turned eighteen. Shombu did get to see Shanti, once before their marriage. It was the day of their engagement ceremony. He stared at her wheatish face for much longer than the protocol warranted. He had stared at girls before and enjoyed his share of fantasies in private, but this was an opportunity for him to have a woman of his own. Shanti's parents lived in a village called Okardaha. They too, like Khagen Das, Shombu's father, came as refugees from Bangladesh in the early 1970's. Shombu was ten at that time.

---

13 Varanasi

It was in the Bengali month of 'Boishak'[14] that Shombu and Shanti looked at each other properly for the first time amongst the sounds of the blowing conch-shells and *Ulu-Dhwani*[15]. Shanti, unveiled her face that she had hid behind the two betel leaves in her hand. It was the moment they would never forget till their last breath; it was their '*Shubho-Drishti*[16]'. It was only after they took their vows of being together through thick and thin, and Shombu following Shanti seven times around the sacred fire, that they were announced as husband and wife. Shanti Mondal became Shanti Das.

It was a hot summer evening in April, when Shanti was welcomed into the Das household. It was a room and a small kitchen. A veranda ran across the length of the room at the entrance. The shack stood in the middle of a slum where the Das's had lived since long. Shombu was eleven when he got here. There was not much in the room, a wooden cot, the four legs of which rested on two bricks each for elevation, couple of wooden cupboards, on the wall on one side was a wooden structure where the Gods rested for long. Among them, was a small framed photograph of Khagen Das. It was decorated with a garland. The room smelled nice, with the fragrance of sandalwood

---

14 Mid April – Mid May

15 Ulu Dhwani refers to a vocal sound made by a group of women. It is not a pan-Indian belief, only certain parts of Eastern India still continue to follow this till today, notably the Bengalis and the Oriyas.

16 Ritual in Bengali marriage where bride and groom look at each other.

incense stick. The neighbours from the nearby shacks had also gathered. An elderly woman said with a mischievous smile to Togorbala, “Now you have to sleep on a mat in the kitchen, else how will you become a grandmother?” There was laughter mostly from the married women who had gathered. Togorbala smiled, Shanti felt embarrassed, Shombu left the room on pretence.

Five years had gone by since that night. A lot had changed in the lives of Shombu and Shanti. They had now learned to live and love each other. The open spaces in the slum had mostly been filled up with new inhabitants, mainly from nearby villages, who had perched themselves there with hope. Togorbala’s photo was now framed and found space next to her husband. They both seemed much happier, with their framed smiles, amidst the company of Gods. Shombu’s income had fallen, going down each year, as they continued their struggle, fuelled with hope.

“One day, everything will be fine, even the rats will come back to torment the households as before, Lord Ganesha[17] probably would have made them stronger and secure,” Shombu would tell Shanti with a smile, replying to most of her complaints on survival. Shanti had now taken reigns of the business of making paper bags from old newspapers. Togorbala had painstakingly taught her the skills, which now helped them with some additional household income.

---

17 Hindu Elephant headed God

There were two things that had remained unchanged in their lives, one, they still did not have electricity in their house and second, they remained childless.

Shanti's mother had brought for them on several occasions, since the last four years, bracelets, twigs, and herbs blessed by religious gurus and tantriks from near and far. She had even given some careful guidance to Shanti, to which Shanti was very embarrassed. They kept working tirelessly, she and Shombu. Some months, when her periods got late, Shombu would look up at her with hope. "Shall we go to the hospital to check?" he would ask. Hope would be crushed, few days later, when he could see Shanti trying to find some old torn sarees. The society did not make it any easier for them. Shanti would find it hard to stand in the queue every morning to fill her buckets with water from the community taps. The women called her barren and unlucky at the slightest provocation in the queue. Some had even stopped allowing her to volunteer to help cooking the meals during the religious occasions. She hid her pain from Shombu, but Shombu read it in her eyes. He would assure her that they would be blessed soon, keeping his hand on the back of her shoulder, as she stood next to the window, quietly looking at the small children playing outside. Shanti, would turn and hide her face in his chest. Shombu would feel the warm drops of tears flowing down, making the hair on his chest wet. He would allow her to finish.

It was an early morning during the first ushers of the monsoon rain, the smell of wet soil was in the air, Shombu opened his eyes to see Shanti staring at him. They were both still lying on the wooden cot, which rested its four legs on two old bricks each. Shombu had never ever woken up seeing Shanti next to him like this. She would have normally begun her daily chores, but that morning, she laid in the bed, half turned waiting for him to wake up. She had a smile in her face, yet her eyes were moist.

"Can you take me to the hospital this morning, I think it may be…," she could not complete, when Shombu nodded his head positively looking back at her. He wiped her tears, which by then had begun to roll down her cheeks. They hugged and continued to lay in bed. It was perhaps too good for both of them to believe, what they both wanted to hear for so long, until the lady doctor at the Imambara Sadar Hospital, told Shanti with assurance, "Yes, you are going to be a mother soon, but you have to be careful and take good care of yourself." They were confused whom to give credit, whether it were the Gods, the bracelets or the black cow that they had fed jaggery and chapatti to every week. Finally, they thanked everyone. Shombu and Shanti felt a sense of accomplishment, they were ecstatic.

They celebrated as if there was no tomorrow. Shombu took his queen to see a Bengali movie. They sat on the wooden chairs towards the front of the screen. Shombu never let go of Shanti's hand all through the movie. Shanti did not want him to take it away either. They had mutton curry and rice, with onions and green chillies on the side in a small road side restaurant before taking a cycle rickshaw back home. They wanted to stay much longer in that moment, but the moon kept moving, to make way for the morning sun.

As Shanti started to observe and feel the changes within her, she could also feel the change around her. No women could now say the same things they had once heaped at her earlier, when she stood in the queue to fill the same buckets with water. Amidst all their new found joys, Shombu and Shanti soon got back to the game of life, trying to answer its questions. They realized within months that they would require more money. Shanti's meagre financial assistance by selling newspaper bags will dwindle soon. Shombu told Shanti, as he lay on the cot, waving a fan made out of palm leaf, that since there were hardly any sales during the weekend, he would start riding cycle rickshaws. He told Shanti, that he already had a chat with his friend Haru, who rode a cycle rickshaw. Haru would soon take him to the money-lender who rented cycle rickshaws.

It was within two weeks that Shombu started riding cycle rickshaw. He quickly learned about the fares, how to bargain, where to park for better fares at different times of the day. The weekend job of riding cycle rickshaw was certainly giving better financial assistance to the household. Months passed by quickly as seasons went by. The lady doctor at the hospital had told Shanti that she should get admitted a day or two before the delivery date, which was towards the middle of March.

The prince arrived without much warning quite ahead of his time, towards the third week of February. There was joy all around, neighbours were flocking in to see a glimpse of the new member of their slum. The eunuchs who lived in the slum had also come in their traditional ways of singing and playing the drums to bless the new born. With great difficulty Shombu got them to leave after having to part with a hundred rupee note. He had offered prayers and pedas[18] at the local temple where the Goddess Kali was worshipped and distributed the pedas to every visitor who had come to see his son. It made him feel like a king giving away gold coins for the occasion.

The wooden cot was not theirs only now, it had to be shared with Shontu, who lay majestically in their middle. Shombu turned staring at Shanti, amidst the faint moon light that entered through the window. She looked at him with a smile as her eyes became moist. They both looked at Shontu, with pride in their eyes. He was theirs, and, they were his.

Shontu's arrival made the Das household even busier. Shombu and Shanti were never happier, they slept less, worked harder and sacrificed more as they fought through

---

18 Sweet dish

the poverty. Shombu had left his job of a salesman, and he rode cycle rickshaws all day till late at night, but always ensured he was home every afternoon, to catch a glimpse of Shontu. Shanti had made a swing using old bedsheets tied to the bamboo rails on which the low ceiling of their asbestos roof rested. She would put her prince there as she made the newspaper bags. She spoke a lot with Shontu, sometimes sang, he became her confidante. Shontu would respond with giggles, squeaks, and occasionally even resisted by crying.

Shontu soon turned one. Shombu would return every night just before dinner and ask Shanti, “Did he say Baba or Ma?” Shanti would respond negatively, nodding her head.

“He is just one,” she would say.

“I started speaking at that age, that is what Ma told me,” he would reply.

Days turned into months, Shontu grew older. Shombu and Shanti continued to yearn to hear the words that they had always dreamt for Shontu to utter. They would think with every passing day when tomorrow would come. Would it be today? Yet that longed for day would always elude them.

Shontu was almost three. He still could not speak. The neighbours passing by would ask Shanti, pointing to Shontu, when they sat at the open veranda of their house, "Still not talking? May be effect of evil spirit or cause of someone's envy, take him to the religious man, in Chinsurah, I am sure he would find a resolve." Their advise had become more frequent and from more people. Shanti had stopped sitting on the veranda with Shontu for longer periods during the day. Her mother would bring her occasional bracelets to be tied to Shontu's forearm from religious men as well as flowers that were offered to the Gods to touch on Shontu's forehead. Shombu had stopped asking Shanti if Shontu had uttered the most coveted words they both wanted to hear so eagerly.

They were puzzled. Life seemed to be taking back slowly what it had given them. Happiness seemed to have been given on loan by time, and it had now come at their doorstep to collect it all back with interest. There were other kids in the neighbourhood who were born around the same time as Shontu. Shanti had known all their mothers and they were a happy bunch together. She could see all those kids, some younger some older than Shontu, running around playing with each other, pestering their mothers to buy them candies and balloons from the salesman who would walk around the slum to sell their wares. They appeared so similar to Shontu. She had always dreamt that she would be pestered as well. She was so lost in her thoughts that she could not even feel the tears rolling down her cheek.

“No I cannot buy you that toy again, money does not grow on trees,” she exclaimed and then realized quickly that she had only reacted to her imagination. She was in her room, amidst newspapers. Shontu sat next to her with a broken plastic red colour car. He was playing with it, watching the wheels as he rolled the car over and over, on the tin walls of the house. He was oscillating and giggling.

“Shontu, stop it, quiet,” Shanti spoke more in anger and frustration than to stop Shontu. He was next to her but seemed unperturbed. She was tired, and was not being able to cope up. It was becoming a full time effort to manage Shontu with every month he was growing physically. He did not seem to understand anything. She was failing to deliver on the quantities of the newspaper bags she was contracted to make for the dealers. There seemed to be sounds of thousands of bells that rang continuously in her mind. She wanted to cry aloud, she wanted to escape, she wanted to give up and accept her defeat in front of the all the Gods that adorned her household. It was always during moments like these that Shontu came and hugged her, as if he read her mind. She looked at him, but his eyes looked away.

They visited every holy and religious man from religions more than one with hope, their savings, and Shontu. Some had even tied up Shontu to a tree in front of a fire where they would offer prayers, flanked by human skulls and bones. It was unbearable for Shanti to look at her helpless son, while such acts were performed, to force the evil spirit, that had made home in Shontu's body out. Shombu acted strong but wept within, as he assured Shanti. The turmoil went on for six months as they travelled far and near, but Shontu's condition remained unaltered as another monsoon ushered.

It was an evening of the Bengali month of *Shrabon*[19], as the rain Gods lashed their fury, Shontu fell very ill. Shombu was not home yet. Shanti got so scared with the temperature that Shontu was running that she called in some of the elderly women from the neighbourhood. They lay around the cot, putting a wet cloth, size of a small handkerchief on his forehead, taking turns. An elderly lady even mentioned in her attempt to console Shanti, before they all left together, "Definitely, it is the effect of the holy man you had visited last week, the evil is coming out, it is a sign, your son will get well and also speak soon, don't worry!" Shanti was silent, she wanted Shombu to come, but the rain Gods were not helping at all.

The lantern that lay on the wooden stool in the corner of the cot where Shontu was lying, was finding it difficult to stay illuminated, as it fought the strong winds and rain. Shanti closed the window with some struggle. She did not want to fight the darkness alone, without Shombu by her side. Shontu was shivering, he was covered with a blanket, the only one they had, but it did not seem to

---

19 July–August

be enough. She got at the two other sarees she had, the extra bed sheet, and even the towels to cover him. At the end, she hugged him hard, in an attempt to give him more comfort and warmth of her body. She had even prayed that along with the heat from the body, the Gods should give her speech to Shontu as well. Shontu had fever before as well, but it was never this bad.

There was a knock on the door. It was Shombu's, she recognized it. Shombu walked in drenched, Shanti, took a towel off Shontu and gave it to Shombu. The father in him looked in despair. He had hardly made any money that day. They sat by Shontu all night. The rain Gods kept pouring, they were relentless in raging fury. "Why us?" Shombu whispered to himself just as the lantern died, only Shanti heard him in the darkness.

The sky was clear the following morning. The rain Gods took some rest after a night of hard work. Shanti woke up to see that Shombu was not in the room. Shontu was still running high temperature, he lay down on the cot weak and hardly being able to open his eyes. Her searching eyes saw Shombu rush into the room.

"I have got the rickshaw, quick, we have to take Shontu to the hospital. You sit on the back and hold him tight, I will ride fast."

Shanti sat on the rickshaw, with Shontu in her arms all wrapped up. The roads in the slum were muddy, as Shombu struggled to push the rickshaw through till he reached the narrow street. He ran and pushed the rickshaw, then jumped on his seat.

"Hold Shontu tight," he said as he pedalled hard putting all his strength in action.

"Do you have any money?" he heard Shanti's voice from behind.

Shombu replied catching his breath at every revolution of the pedal, "Taken some money in the morning, from the owner of the rickshaw."

They reached the hospital. There were more like them, poor and needy, in a huge queue of the General Ward of the government hospital. They waited anxiously while praying hard. Shombu occasionally left Shanti alone, much to her anger to smoke a few beedis[20] and also catch a quick glimpse of his rickshaw that was parked in one corner of the hospital. Finally their turn came.

The doctor examined Shontu. He asked him to show his tongue. Shontu did not even seem to hear him from so close, he quickly looked away from the doctor, avoiding eye contact. The doctor asked him his name as he tried to communicate with Shontu. He moved his stethoscope over his chest. Shontu was becoming increasingly restless and in the absence of speech, could only express himself by crying. Shanti managed him and carried him in her

---

20 Cigarette for the poor, tobacco wrapped in a tendu or temburni leaf (plants native to Asia) and may be secured with a colourful string at one or both ends.

arms to pacify him, while the doctor sat down in his chair, keeping the stethoscope on his table.

"All vaccinations up to date, show me the file?" The doctor asked Shombu while writing a prescription without even looking at Shombu, who sat uncomfortably in a chair in front of the doctor across the table.

"Yes," said Shombu, passing the file which had all the necessary documents since the day Shontu was born in the same hospital. Shanti had kept each one of them carefully stored in that file, hospital card, immunization card and others, even the medical bills. She used to keep the file in her wooden cupboard at home in the bottom drawer.

The doctor, who appeared to be in his mid-fifties, examined the documents in the file, gazing through his reading glasses which were balanced perfectly on the edge of his nose. He occasionally made a grunt while turning the pages. Shanti looked at Shombu, worried and anxious. She stood next to him with Shontu in her arms, as he rested his head on his mother's shoulder.

"Here, some medicines, see these are free, which I have put in this white small envelope, you have to buy this tonic from the pharmacy, he will be fine in 5 to 6 days, give him lot of water and plain and simple khichudi[21], no spice," the doctor explained looking at Shombu. Shombu and Shanti looked little relieved, and as a smile was about to appear on their faces, the doctor continued, "But..." He

21 A dish from the Indian subcontinent made from rice and lentils

paused, longer than that was required between two words, removed his glasses, and leaned forward, resting his arms on the table.

"The problem what I fear is somewhere else with your son," he continued.

"What sir?" Shombu asked as anxiety eclipsed his smile.

"I suspect he has a problem, in the working of his brain, he may be Autistic," doctor said.

"He is not mad, he is ok," Shanti tried defending her son, Shombu could not understand anything. He looked helplessly at the doctor and asked quietly, "He will be cured, right?"

The doctor gave him a letter and asked them to take Shontu to a Child Psychologist in the same hospital, but did not answer Shombu. Shombu and Shanti thanked the doctor and left his room in silence. Shombu rode through the busy streets with Shanti sitting behind, Shontu in her arms. They heard their silence amidst the hustle and bustle of the busy narrow streets of the small town, as Shombu rode on. None, but probably the pigeons sitting on the overhead electric cables saw the tears that rolled through the cheeks of Shombu. They rolled down to meet the sweat on his face at the edge of the jaw line. He looked up towards the sky in search of someone, but the Gods were not there.

Shontu recovered in a week and they visited the Child Psychologist after that. They waited for their turn in silence, while managing Shontu, taking turns. They did not understand most of the things the psychologist explained. They only remembered that the young lady had said that Shontu's condition is a disorder and not a disease. He would need a lot of therapies for which they have to go weekly to Kolkata, and it will be expensive. She told them to be positive and hopeful as they left her room. Shombu, stopped and turned just before he was about to step out of her room with Shontu by his side, holding his hand, he looked at her for a split second, then moved on. There were a lot of questions in that look, but he asked none. He felt as if someone had kept a heavy stone on his chest, a lump generated in his voice.

Shanti climbed at the back of the rickshaw, Shontu sat next to her as Shanti held on to him. The wheels turned as Shombu pedalled, it was a beautiful day, but he and Shanti were numb. Shontu was looking around, probably at the world, trying to find his spot. He was happy, totally oblivious to the way the world looked at him.

Twelve years went by since that day. Shontu had now almost become an adult. He was seventeen but remained childlike in his demeanour. Shombu and Shanti had taken Shontu once a week to Howrah to a Government hospital for therapies till the age of ten, but could not afford after that. They would start at dawn, walk for 30 minutes to the station, take a train, then a crowded bus, managing Shontu. He would cry for survival in those crowded buses, much to the annoyance of the passengers. Some understood, most did not, some even inflicted torments like, “Why do you have to board a bus with a mentally retarded child?” Shontu struggled, while Shombu and Shanti swallowed every insult in silence. There were many like them in the hospital, some even had money.

Shombu tried hard to manage the weekly sixty five rupees that was required for Shontu’s therapy at the hospital. Fifty rupees was a fee he had to pay at the hospital, the rest was spent on travel and food. It was almost two days of his earning. He had taken a loan, and sold all of Shanti’s jewellery to pay it off along with interest to the local loan sharks in the last seven years. It had been almost five years since Shanti lost her income from making newspaper bags. Plastic was all round, and replaced most things from money to newspaper bags.

No matter how hard he pedalled, Shombu never seemed even close to win his race against life. He would look at Shontu, sitting on the veranda outside the entrance of their house, through the half opened door and think, he was already earning money and contributing to the household at Shontu’s age. It was the rule, why did the Gods change it for him. His earnings kept dropping each year as commuters looked for speed and used more of automobile rickshaws or autos, than cycle rickshaw. He also could not pedal as quickly as before. He and Shanti both looked much older than their age. They saved most of the rice for Shontu, while relying mostly on the starch and little rice that remained for them.

Shanti worked hard to teach Shontu ways to survive. Shombu would ask her late in the night, while lying on the floor amidst darkness, "Will he be able to live without us?" He never got an answer from Shanti. He used to wait for a while then turn around and sleep, thinking that Shanti had fallen asleep already. Shanti could hear him snore as she stared into the darkness, lying on the cot next to her son.

He ran pillar to post to manage aid from the local NGO's, but could not get any. Some would think he is cooking up stories, others would come and tell him to put him to mental hospital, which were free of cost and supported by Government. He wanted to rebel against the whole world and even fight the Gods. He just didn't want to lose his only child.

It was a cold winter evening couple of months before Shontu's eighteenth birthday, Shombu returned home much earlier than usual. He looked very pale and sat down on the cot. Shontu was sitting on the floor next to his mother, talking gibberish while turning the pages of an old Bengali newspaper. He looked at his father and kept repeating Baba, while oscillating his body back and forth till Shanti stopped him. Shanti noticed blood stains on the left sleeve of the ash coloured full sweater that Shombu was wearing. It had holes in a few places in the back. Shombu realized that Shanti had observed it. He asked for water and quickly stepped outside onto the open veranda. Shanti heard him cough as he poured water in a steel glass, inside. Shontu was clapping his hands as he kept repeating "Baba." Shanti rushed out on the veranda with the glass of water and saw Shombu squatting on one corner and spitting cough. Shombu turned quickly to face her, seeing her shadow falling over him in front. He looked at her eyes, she handed him the glass and rushed in. Shombu followed her. He sat next to her on the wooden cot.

The lantern was flickering, cold breeze was coming in through the window, which though closed, had gaps at the bottom where the two wooden frames closed in. He held her hand and she hid her face in his chest, crying aloud. He allowed her to cry as he told her, that he had hidden his condition from her, for the past several months. He had gone to see the doctor at the hospital that day, who told him he will have at best three or four months to live. He told Shanti that it was getting very difficult for him to ride the cycle rickshaw. He told her that she should now start looking for a job while he can be at home to look after Shontu. Shanti looked up, still sobbing, and questioned, "And what after three months or at best the fourth?"

Shanti found it difficult to close her eyes that night. While Shontu and Shombu were sleeping on the wooden cot, she lay wide awake on the floor, staring at the darkness.

Her whole life flashed past in front of her, as if she was seeing a movie in a large dark auditorium all by herself. She asked herself if she would be able to live her life all alone with Shontu, without Shombu by her side. She could feel her eyelids getting heavy. They closed on her eyes as darkness prevailed.

Shanti found herself jobs with two households as a maid with the help of her friend Batashi, who lived in the same slum. Shanti had to clean the utensils, sweep the floor and wash the clothes. She started early in the morning and would return around lunch time. She would come back to see father and son, engaged, keeping each other's company. Shombu was making the best use of his time by not being conscious of it. He had started to count his days backwards and would remind Shanti with every passing day of the count. The Das family seemed to be happy, as if they had found their plenty among poverty. They were happy each moment that they were together. They would even go out every Sunday evening to stroll by the Ganges. They had never realized earlier how close the river was from where they lived. Sometimes when you could see the end, you could look straight into the eyes of time and tell that you would like to enjoy every moment of what remained.

It was the afternoon of Shontu's eighteenth birthday when Shanti got back home. She had a small packet of laddoo[22], a sweet that Shontu was so fond of. There was something else also in her hand, it was a small packet, which she quickly hid inside her blouse and fixed her saree. Shombu enthusiastically took the packet from her hands and quickly opened it to find three orange coloured laddoos. Shanti took them away from him and said we will have it in the evening. She would use it as a cake to celebrate Shontu's birthday. Shanti suggested they should go for a walk by the river Ganges that evening. They sat on the banks of the river, Shanti, Shontu, and Shombu. Shombu coughed a bit more that evening as it reminded him of something. He told Shanti while looking at the river Ganges in front that as per his count, it was the last day of his three month period. He was not scared as he spoke. It was his way of taking leave. Shanti did not react. She told him that she had lost her job with the two households as they came to know that her husband was suffering from tuberculosis. There was neither fear nor anxiety as she spoke. The seemed like two banks, separated by a river that was Shontu. They held his hands and continued to watch the river.

They sat down in a circle after dinner. They had celebrated Shontu's birthday well with two packets of mutton biryani, which they shared and enjoyed. Shanti had lit a small thin candle in the middle of the circle, next to it was the packet of laddoos. The room was dark around

22 Indian sweet made from a mixture of flour, sugar, and shortening, which is shaped into a ball.

them. Shanti carefully took out the small packet from her blouse and gave it to Shombu. Shombu recognized the packet, it was Jibon brand, he looked at Shanti, mixed it well in the three laddoos. Shontu kept repeating, "Baba, Ma" looking at them both. They kissed him and wished him. Shombu offered one to Shanti. He fed Shontu one himself with great care. They then looked at each other, the same way as they did during their *Shubho Dristhi*. They put their laddoos in their mouth. They chewed on it as they smiled, while tears rolled down. They could not see Shontu struggle next to them, but heard him cry loudly in pain and then faintly, till they heard nothing. The candle flickered one last time with all its brightness, before darkness filled the room.

The Smoke Ring Man

The door closed mildly as Aditya walked down couple of short steps onto a narrow lane. There was an air of sadness; he was not sure whether he would ever walk through that door back again, which closed behind him. He knew there was someone standing in the balcony as he walked on. He stopped and turned back within a few paces, to look up behind towards the balcony. He could only see a hand waving out through the grill of the balcony, they were covered by the white sleeves of a cotton Kurta[23].

A chain of smoke rings followed quickly, moving past the hand to disappear into the air between the two houses across the narrow lane. Aditya could not see the face of that hand nor the creator of the smoke rings. He knew it was *the smoke ring man*. He raised his hand in acknowledgement as he walked on looking ahead, as the *smoke ring man* saw his friend disappear. He knew, the *smoke ring man* was happy. A happiness that he as a mere mortal, ordinary soul tied to finite material goals would never ever understand.

---

23 Indian cotton shirt, ethnic home wear

Debraj was not always the smoke ring man. He was different, sublime in nature, and eccentrically brilliant. Aditya lit a cigarette, as the non-air-conditioned yellow cab drove through the streets of Kolkata, honking relentlessly. He could have called an air-conditioned cab, much more comfortable using his fancy Pixel phone, but chose not to. He felt that a lot of things in this city remained the same as it were thirty years back. Debraj and he were in the final year of their high school then. It were the same yellow cabs, they would sometimes ride along with a few other friends, pooling in money to pay for the ride, passing a common cigarette around, as each took turns for their share of puff. They could only afford to buy one cigarette pooling some spare changes. It was more of an act of experiencing the guilt and a symbolic attempt to prove that they were on the steps of manhood. As the cool breeze hit his face, Aditya felt so desperate to escape back to those days, wear his school uniform, sling his school back around and meet Debraj, Partha, Ari—his circle of friends.

"I never thought I would ever venture out of this neighbourhood," Aditya murmured to himself as he sipped his whisky, standing on the terrace of his father's three story house. The sun was setting on the horizon amidst the high rises, not sure how it even found space, each day to set and then rise, to wake up the city. It was his last evening in the city, before he went back to his home. The parameter of 'Home' had a new value parsed now. It was Sydney.

Aditya had been living there for the past twenty years. He met Debraj in this trip to Kolkata after almost twenty four years. He had last seen him a week after Debraj, as expected, was selected to join the most premiere engineering institute in India. He was very happy for him. Debraj had told him that time, "Don't worry, you will find a seat somewhere also." Yes that somewhere was certainly found, and Aditya had left for Down South of India to explore his destiny. He wondered why they had not seen each other; rather Aditya had never remembered Debraj much after that. It was not until six months back when through a common friend, Aditya could find out about Debraj, on a social media platform. He was extremely happy.

That night came back to him vividly. He was in his study, working late, responding to irritating work emails. His wife Susmita was busy putting the dishes from dinner into the dishwasher. As a moment of escape, Aditya had turned to the social media site, through some serendipity, located Debraj through a post of another friend who had tagged him. Debraj seemed to look pretty much the same as he did when they had last met. He had sent him a friend request along with a message that night, and mentioned he would be reaching Kolkata in a couple of weeks. He had shouted from his study to Susmita in Bengali, "Found him! Found him!" Susmita was confused and annoyed, as it was with great difficulty she could force their eight-year-old son Jojo to sleep.

Aditya could not stop thinking about Debraj, as his flight started it's ascend. It had now soared into the Australian sky, onwards his home, leaving Kolkata and Debraj far behind. Success, or so called material success as defined by middle class Bengali families, which included parameters as education, job, rather overseas job, NRI[24] status, wife, children, house, and a luxury car, had found him. The questions that he continually asked himself, as his plane soared higher and higher invading through the covers of cloud into the night sky, were, "What now? Am I happy? What is happiness? Is success happiness or is happiness success?" He seemed to have no answers for any of them. He began to feel uncomfortable in his Business class seat as the questions kept echoing in his mind.

Aditya was content being in the bottom ten percent of his class. His strategy had always been enough to avoid the red ink on the report card. He had the qualities of being a good salesman from those days, thick skinned to all his father's rebuke and sometimes even disregard a slap or two from him.

Aditya had never thought he would find Debraj in Kolkata. He was an icon back in the school days, everybody else seemed to have decided what they wanted

---

24 Non Resident Indian

him to become. Graduation, with highest ranks, move to the promised land, United States of America, with a lucrative scholarship, Masters and PhD from an Ivy League University, and finally the coveted Professor. Debraj had crushed all their dreams and chose happiness as his destination. It takes someone as brave as him to choose such a destination. He had won it over all of them again, this time, graduating with highest honours from the University of Life.

It was only in Sydney Airport, moments before Aditya boarded his flight to Kolkata that he saw Debraj had accepted his friend request. Debraj had even sent him a message and shared his mobile number. He could not stop thinking about Debraj and their meeting since they had parted as schoolmates.

Aditya walked up toward Debraj, as he saw him enter the coffee shop. "How are you?" Aditya exclaimed embracing Debraj. In the mirror, in front of them, the guests could see two six-year-olds meeting in their school uniform, just the way they had met for the first time. It seemed that they had never been separated. Debraj looked at Aditya and smiled.

"You have not changed," Debraj said.

"Changed a lot," Aditya replied, pointing to his beer belly and hair that had started to grey out, as they sat down.

"Ready to order sir?" the waiter asked in a manner befitting the ambience of the coffee shop of the five-star hotel.

"Flat white, no sugar for me," Aditya replied and immediately and saw a confused expression on the waiter's face, and quickly corrected himself. "Normal coffee with milk, and no sugar."

"Black coffee," Debraj said smiling at the waiter. "So looks like you have made it quite big in the Corporate World of Sydney, well done!"

"You tell me, you would be a multi-millionaire now, sitting on a score of patents, entourage of cars and countless property?" Aditya spoke.

"None of the above," Debraj replied with a smile, leaning back in his chair, looking around the vast but sparsely occupied coffee shop of the five-star hotel.

"Come on, I can't believe this," Aditya responded with an honest sense of relief deep in his heart. He felt nice to have scored higher than his friend in this important exam of life.

"Where have you reached?" Debraj enquired.

The waiter arrived to serve them coffee. Aditya was waiting for this moment to share his journey of success. He started from his current position and went back till the time they had drifted away. He told Debraj about his four bedroom house in Dee Why, its proximity to the beach, his swimming pool, size of his lawn, two cars, his wife and son. He had it all. The child in him was running with a balloon in the hand all around the coffee shop, wearing a victorious smile. He asked his friend, "Wife? Kids?" Debraj replied with a smile, "No kids, no wife." Aditya smiled.

The airhostess came and interrupted his thoughts to ask if he wanted anything to drink or eat. Aditya replied negatively in an urgency to get back to his thoughts. He did not want to miss the moment.

"What are you doing now, tell me everything since we last met!" Aditya remembered asking Debraj in the coffee shop.

"I thought we would have met at the small tea shop near Park Circus, our old spot. Tea is now five rupees there, it was about one rupee when we had last been there together. I can tell with your choice of venue that you surely have become a cliché NRI, are you drinking mineral water at home here?" Debraj responded with a chuckle.

"Let's meet at our old haunt tomorrow, but tell me what are you busy in life with?" Aditya pressed on.

"Are you happy?" Debraj asked. There was a pause as Aditya gathered his answer. He replied with a smile that took a bit of effort to appear. "Why not? I have everything I had wanted? You are not answering my question."

"If you really want to know, would you come with me to Ramnagar tomorrow? We will be back the following day. It is a place near Digha, we take the 7 a.m. train from Howrah station," Debraj asked.

Aditya had travelled without his family for this trip. Although it was a business trip, he wanted to see his ageing parents as well. But he could not let go of his corporate habits, he quickly checked his calendar on the phone. "Nothing in the calendar tomorrow, it's Saturday, so surely I will come along. Will you organize fermented coloured water for the night?"

It was 6:45 a.m., the train was lazily making its way into the platform where Aditya and Debraj stood. Aditya was feeling an excitement from within. Years back when he and Debraj were in class eleven, they had taken a train to Bandel to go for a picnic with a few more friends. He felt very light and happy. He asked Debraj as the train settled on the platform in front of them, "Coach number? Seat number?"

Debraj did not respond. He seemed a bit absent minded. He looked at his watch and then towards the entrance of the platform where scores of people kept entering. He was trying to call someone without much luck. It was a busy platform, extremely noisy. Families going for a weekend trip, hawkers trying to sell things to them, porters trying to bargain, and amidst all this, Aditya could notice Debraj's eyes searching desperately for someone. Aditya suddenly noticed a smile at the corner of Debraj's lips. "Here, here, this way? Hurry! Hurry, this way." Debraj spoke enthusiastically, as he led his friends through the crowd. They scampered onto their air-conditioned chair car compartment.

"Anindita, you sit here by the window, Aditya you seat there," Debraj said as he sat next to Anindita, pointing to the aisle seat next to him across the passage. Aditya had thought that it would only be him and Debraj. Now there was Anindita, and certainly she was quite important getting to sit next to Debraj, and that too the window seat. Aditya recalled Debraj telling him the previous evening that he was not married.

"Who is this woman?" Aditya thought as he turned towards Anindita with a smile. The train left the platform as the passengers settled in.

Debraj and Aditya were both in their early forties, Anindita did not seem much younger to them. As questions were flying around Aditya's mind on Anindita's identity and her relation with Debraj, Debraj interrupted his thoughts and introduced her.

Anindita was an attractive woman, though not on the taller side. She was neither fat nor athletic. She was smiling and seemed carefully careless. She had draped a saree, red and gold in floral pattern with carefully chosen ethnic jewellery. The winner was her nose ring. Her glasses gave her the intellectual look, without diluting her attraction quotient. Aditya would have liked a red dot on her empty forehead though. She seemed to be very comfortable in the company of Debraj.

Anindita leaned forwarded a bit for an eye contact with Aditya and spoke, "Hello, is this is your first trip to Ramnagar?"

"First trip!" replied Aditya with a nod.

"You will enjoy it, it is different from your Sydney," Anindita replied.

Debraj would have told her about him, thought Aditya. Is she his girlfriend, wondered Aditya, still not very convinced. Anindita deserved someone more successful, he thought.

"Where do you live in Kolkata?" asked Aditya.

"I live near Gol Park, when I am in Kolkata. It is only 2-3 months in a year, mostly January – March. Rest of the time I'm in US, Livonia, a small city close to Detroit," replied Anindita

Aditya smiled, trying best not to show his curiosity. "I am sure Livonia is also different to Ramnagar?" he said and turned to lookat Debraj. "What is there in Ramnagar? What are we going to do there?"

"Will be revealed in due course," Anindita replied with a smile and then looked at Debraj. A hawker who was selling puffed rice mixed with onion, spices, mustard oil, chillies, dried coconut, lemon juice, and peanuts, was passing by as Anindita pressed on Debraj. "Quick order, before he disappears," and then addressed Aditya as Debraj hailed the hawker, "I am sure this will do no harm to you."

She seemed to be at ease. Aditya wanted to ask her how.

"Bit more chilli in mine," Anindita chirped to the hawker. Debraj looked at her with a smile. Aditya noticed the care in Debraj's face.

"Enough chilli for you?" Debraj enquired as he paid the hawker.

Anindita nodded in satisfaction as she devoured yet another chilli in the puffed rice mixture. She sweated in the air-conditioned compartment. Aditya inquired, whilst chewing the puffed rice, amidst the sounds of mastication and crunchiness, "What do you do?"

"Nothing much, more of a housewife, benefit of having a well to do husband," Anindita replied spontaneously. Debraj was sitting in the middle of them, he looked at Aditya. He had half a smile on his lips, his eyes wanted to plead, ask nothing more please. The train sped on, going past the lush green fields and stations which were not important in its path. The sun fell strongly on the window as Anindita pulled the curtain. Aditya saw Debraj had fallen asleep. He was not sure if he was sleeping or closed his eyes to avoid any potential interrogation from Aditya. The train had reached Tamluk when Aditya looked at this watch, another hour and half before they would reach Ramnagar. He reclined his seat, placed his hands comfortably on his beer belly and gazed at the meshed ceiling fan, as it rotated tirelessly. It took him back to their carefree school days.

"We have to take the next bus now, it has been more than an hour that we are having an aimless adda[25]," Debraj shouted at Aditya as they waited at the bus terminus, near their school in Park Circus in Kolkata. "They are all pretty crowded, wait for another half an hour and we will get an empty bus," Aditya replied. He continued complaining. "You did not show me anything today, my Physics exam has gone for a toss!"

"Don't be greedy, you copied the last two answers from me," Debraj said indifferently.

"I changed the variables, where you had x and y, I used d and e," Aditya replied with pride.

"I am getting into this bus, I have got a lot to study for Chemistry exam tomorrow," said Debraj as he jumped into the bus. He squeezed himself through the S14[26], on its way to Garia. He seemed bit relieved at the thought that Aditya probably had not been able to board the bus.

---

25 Conversation in Bengali

26 Bus number

"Yes, I forgot, is it Chemistry tomorrow?" Aditya chirped to Debraj's surprise, standing next to him, while trying to organize his bag. "Here two Gariahat," he continued as he bought the tickets from the conductor. "Bought your ticket," he said further turning towards Debraj.

"Does not matter, I will not show you anything tomorrow," Debraj responded. Aditya squeezed his cheek and replied, "You are too kind, what is the use of both of us studying the same thing?" The bus braked suddenly.

It woke Aditya up from his dream. He got his chair in the upright position, looked around and wondered how did he get into that train. He saw Debraj next to him. He seemed to have grown much older to the boy he met moments back. His mobile suddenly rang, as he pulled out the phone from the seat pocket. He could see in the reflection of the screen as the phone rang, the face of a man, who had mustache and a French beard, surely this was not Aditya.

"Susmita, how are you? How is Jojo?" Aditya spoke. Susmita gave him all the updates as he did his.

Anindita had woken up, she looked at Aditya speaking on the phone, smiled as she was trying to fix her sari, ensuring it covered her cleavage.

"Wify?" Anindita asked as Aditya finished his phone call. He nodded his head. "Both of you slept a lot, now wake up the King of Gods," Aditya said. Anindita pushed Debraj a few times before he finally woke up. Aditya could feel a sense of ownership from the way Anindita woke Debraj up. He wanted to define the relationship, but struggled. Surely, with all these years in the Western world, he had remained a typical rice eating Bong[27].

The train reached Ramnagar. It was just before noon, sun was scorching, as the three of them stood in the desolate platform. Aditya stretched himself and then looked around. He reached for his packet of cigarette from the front flap of his rucksack. He lit a Gold flake, and felt very satisfied with its first puff, exhaling smoke that appeared as a steam engine coming out from his nose. He saw in a distance, Debraj talking to two men. They seemed to be local and were obediently nodding their heads with a smile to whatever, Debraj was telling them. Anindita was standing next to Debraj. They looked good together.

Debraj yelled, "Come, there is a car outside."

It was 6 p.m. in the two-storey house in Ramnagar. Debraj was in a room that was occupied by 8 desktop computers and 16 enthusiastic teenagers of Ramnagar, 10 boys and 6 girls. They were sharing the desktops, without any complain, eagerly absorbing every word that Debraj spoke. Aditya stood in a corner, observing the kids of Ramnagar being prepared to face the Global platform of Information Technology. There were women in the house,

---

27 Bengali

who were being taught how to make handicrafts as well. Debraj was so sought after, everyone wanted a piece of him. Aditya felt lonely even among a myriad of people. He watched Anindita as she worked tirelessly with the women, there was so much of intent, there was so much of care, and there was so much of happiness. They seemed to be in a flow, Debraj and Anindita.

Aditya pondered for a moment, as he stood alone on the dimly lit empty terrace of the house, what would be the best way to define the relationship between the man and the woman of the moment. His thoughts were disturbed when a middle aged man came to serve him tea. Friendship was perhaps that definition, he acknowledged with a smile, gazing at the stars in the night sky, as he sipped the tea.

The small unnoticeable house in the corner of a weakly lit town seemed to perhaps be the best institution of hope in the world at that moment. There was a smile and hope in every face that Debraj engaged. He was indeed their resurrection man. He felt a hand on his shoulder, it was Debraj.

"Sorry, just could not get time to find out how you are doing in the middle of all this commotion," asked Debraj. Aditya looked at Debraj, with eyes that were moist but full of pride for his friend. He wanted to say something to Debraj, when Anindita shouted from the doorway of the terrace, “Khichudi[28] and fried Hilsa Fish waiting to be served steaming hot, coming down you two.”

“Be there in five, finishing a well-deserved smoke,” replied Debraj. A chain of smoke rings came out, between his lips to disappear into the sky, below which lay the land of hope. “Let’s, drive up to the beach after dinner,” Debraj said, stubbing off the cigarette under his slippers.

It was one of the best dinners Aditya had in a long time, thirty people sat on the floor, being served on banana leaves and water in clay glasses. He did not want to leave the place. There were constraints, but amidst all that existed peace, simplicity, and happiness.

Debraj and Aditya left for the beach in a motor cycle shortly after dinner, which Debraj rode. Anindita stayed back, she wanted the friends to talk. It felt like two teenagers riding off into the darkness of night. They reached the beach. Debraj lit a cigarette with a bit of difficulty, battling the strong winds. Aditya saw a sense of satisfaction in Debraj’s face, in that fraction of a second, that the lighter light. His friend was beyond all measurements of success, certainly much beyond his imagination of a successful and wealthy professor settled in USA. The two friends sat on a boulder, heard the waves lash, shared periodic puffs from one cigarette that made its red tip create a prominent glow invading the dark night. They did not talk much, but their silence communicated with each other.

---

28 A mix of rice and lentils cooked together with herbs and spices, popular Bengali cuisine

"What do you think of my work?" Debraj asked breaking the silence. Aditya rose, looked at Debraj, hugged him and said, "Same as I felt about your work during our school days. Brilliant."

Aditya felt the cool sea breeze on his face as he rode the motor cycle back from the beach. Debraj sat behind him. It felt like they were still in their high school. Aditya had desperately wanted time to stop. He wanted to ask a lot of things to Debraj, why he choose this path, his future, and about Anindita, but chose not to.

He had everything that a mere mortal could desire for—a house, a beautiful family, money in the bank, great career—yet he felt a void. He imagined sitting in his business class seat, rings of smoke slowly coming out of the grills of a balcony, and then a sleeve of a white cotton full sleeved kurta, as it hanged out through the grill, fingers holding the cigarette. He felt like escaping. The pilot made an announcement to fasten seat belt due to bad weather. Aditya fastened his seat belt. There was a sound of a click as the seat belt secured itself. Aditya was now tied, but did not feel secure.

East Bengal Kitchen

Like every day the crows had arrived very punctually at the stroke of eight o'clock for their morning ritual. There were four of them that perched on the railing of the balcony equidistant from each other that waited very patiently. The fat Marwari elderly housewife entered the balcony. She had a few chapattis[29] in her left hand. They were left over from previous night's dinner. She raised her right hand to scare the crows, but they remain perched, undeterred. It was only after a couple of attempts that one of the crows took off signalling the others to follow, failing which their breakfast would be delayed. They balanced themselves on the electric cables that ran over the narrow street separating their breakfast area and an unpainted house behind them. The fat woman now quickly made small bite size pieces of the chapattis, while responding to a voice that came from inside. It was of her husband. She left, keeping the pieces of chapatti on the railing, carefully lining them up. The crows delightfully took off for another breakfast of their lives.

Brototi stood watching them and the fat lady from the balcony of the unpainted house. She had been watching

29 Flat bread

the same act with a childlike enthusiasm every morning since the last five years. She quietly smiled but had to hide it by covering her mouth with the edge of her saree. As most mornings, her thoughts were interrupted by the voice of Kundo, when she shouted from below to open the door. Brototi could see Kundo through the grills of her balcony as she waited in front of the door. Like every day, she put the small grocery bag down through the grill of her balcony that had the keys to the door. Brototi set this process up since the last couple years. It saved her from climbing down from her first floor apartment to open the door of the main entrance to her house. Kundo would come up and keep the key back in that bag; it was the duplicate set of keys. She would then get busy washing the utensils and the clothes later, while Brototi would make tea for both. After that she would sit on dinning chair right in front of the kitchen and read the Bengali newspaper while sipping her tea, occasionally informing Kundo on the important headlines of the morning.

"What can the poor do, we have to accept everything without daring to open our mouths, is this life? Death is much better than this!" was the standard response from Kundo most days, while sweeping the floor with occasional sighs of despair to add to the melodrama.

Bratati enjoyed this part of her day very much. She could at least hear a voice, and was not alone. Kundo would finish her work and leave around 11:30 a.m. every day. She had been living by herself for the last four years since the demise of her husband. Brototi's son had on numerous occasions pleaded her to come and live with him in Austin, Texas, where he worked as a software engineer. Brototi had refused each one of those requests. She had told Ranjan that she would not be comfortable living away from the house that his father had built for them. Ranjan had never told her that he would come back to live with her. She had always yearned to hear those words. She could not imagine living in a foreign land at her age of sixty-two. She had visited Ranjan once with her husband. It was for a month.

"Would you not like to live here forever?" her husband had asked her jokingly then.

"It is beautiful, but too lonely for my liking," she had responded.

It was indeed lonely now, but she was not alone. The people in the neighbourhood were around. The streets were busy and buzzing, never mind if they were narrow and not the cleanest.

The days in her life passed by, but they were all the same. She was breathing, but not necessarily living. Her daily routine never changed. She would visit the evening market every alternate day to do her shopping. They would include vegetables, fish, groceries, and household items. Ranjan had always advised his mother to use a particular mobile application to order everything to save her from going out. He had bought her a smartphone when he visited couple of years back, and taught her how to use it. She used it extensively to video chat with Ranjan, but would never learn to use the apps that would make her a prisoner in her own house. It was her escape. She would return around 7 p.m. listening to the sounds of the conch-shells that floated from some of the houses in the neighbourhood. She would come back, stack up her groceries, cook, eat, watch television, and fall asleep to wake up the following morning to meet the crows. She needed a purpose in her life.

There was one other thing that she awaited eagerly every Friday afternoon. It was her meeting with Srabonti. They would have lunch together. Srabonti would spend the afternoon with her younger sister and leave around 5 p.m. after having the afternoon tea that was served with toast biscuits. The sisters would dip them in their tea till it became soggy, and eat them just at the point they were to drop into the tea. They appeared as children who had refused to accept adulthood.

Srabonti was couple of years older to Brototi, but appeared younger. She was very different to Brototi not only in appearance, but also her approach to life. She was taller and slender of the two sisters. Srabonti had worked for over thirty years in a multi-national company in finance, while Brototi had been a dedicated homemaker. Brototi wore shades of white while Srabonti never wore white.

Srabonti was married, her husband now retired as well. Their only son Santanu was married. She also had a five year old grandson. They all lived together in their small two bed room apartment not far from Brototi's house.

Srabonti and Hemandra had bought the apartment with a lot of sacrifice and challenges. They had always hoped that their small apartment that they shared with their son, daughter-in-law, and grandson, would be their palace of happiness. They had wished that once they had retired they would go out and see their state, their country, and perhaps a bit of the world outside their country. They would let Santanu and Sutapa take the ownership of the household chores. They would in return allow them to wear their wings to fly. It had not happened. Santanu and Sutapa both worked in large multi-national software companies, they earned enough money to buy their own apartment of the same size, but they did not. Santanu had always cited his love for his parents and hence could not imagine the thought of living away from them. The truth was a lot different, here the benefits were much greater. They did not have to bother about any household responsibilities, breakfast till dinner was available without any of their effort. They could sleep late and had even outsourced the care of their son. Hemandra would drop his grandson in the morning to kindergarten and finish the daily shopping of vegetables, poultry or fish on his way back. Srabonti would be right on time about mid-day to pick up Joy, bring him back home, feed him, read out stories, and take care of him till his parents came back home to shower their love on him. They felt like prisoners in their own household.

Srabonti could not even remember when they had a meal together as a family. She had always hoped that they would all go out together in one of the evenings during Durga Pujo after seeing some idols for a nice continental dinner. It never happened. Santanu and Sutapa had packed schedules with their friends, they would take Joy along as well. The response from Santanu would always be that it is a time of the year that his parents should spend time with each other and relax. They work so hard all year round. It was the time of the year when Srabonti and Hemandra could avail their annual leaves. It seemed that they were also just breathing, and not living. She too waited eagerly for her Friday afternoon meeting with Brototi. Hemandra had suggested this to her, as he looked after Joy, while she was away.

The sisters would eat their lunch together and often continue their conversation without washing their hands till they would feel the dried lentils or curry on their fingers. Brototi always made sure that she had prepared the tomato chutney with finely chopped ginger for her elder sister. It was her favourite. Srabonti would keep taking small helps of the same with a tea spoon even after she had finished eating her lunch. It made their conversation more exciting. Brototi would prepare most dishes from Eastern part of the once un-divided Bengal. Their parents had migrated from there many years ago. The sisters would often hear stories from their mother while she was busy cooking, how things were better for them on the other side. She would complain of most things about the city they had migrated then, from adulterated mustard oil to fresh produce, and of course the fish.

Brototi had developed a liking for cooking from her mother. She was an expert hand from cooking banana flowers or 'mocha' in Bengali to sukto[30] to fish paturi to mutton kosha. This was a key skill that was always highlighted to prospective grooms when her parents were looking for a match for her. Srabonti on the other hand did not rely on her parents. She had found Hemandra by herself. He also lived in the same neighbourhood in Jadavpur. Her parents objected a little, but were happy to give their consent as Hemandra was from the same caste as theirs, educated with a job, and most importantly also hailed from East Bengal.

It was one such Friday afternoon, towards the middle of November, when the sisters had finished their lunch, but kept chatting without washing their hands. The fingers on their right hand were getting dry and they were scrubbing of the lentils and some grains of rice sticking with their thumb. There was a moment of silence before Srabonti exhaled.

---

30 Light and less spicy mixed vegetable curry

"There needs to be a purpose in our lives, it cannot only be taking care of grandkids and cooking, a sacrificing self forever."

"You are right Didi!" Brototi had responded and then continued as she cleared the plates. "What else can we do? Especially at this age, we just have to accept things as they are I guess."

She kept the plates in the sink of her kitchen after clearing the fish bones and some leftovers in the garbage bin.

"Why? We are strong. There is a lot we can do besides thinking of ourselves as vegetables," Srabonti replied as she washed her hands at the wash basin in the corner of the dining area.

She heard her sister laugh from the kitchen as she wiped her hands on the towel that was hanging from a small round towel rail right next to the wash basin. She took a moment to fix her hair with her hands looking at the mirror above the washing basin and adjusted the red dot on her forehead as well before she spoke again.

"We can do a lot, it is only if we desire to. What age are you talking about?"

Brototi brought a bottle that contained roasted fennel seeds and offered it to Srabonti.

"Really!" She said with a smile.

The sisters lay down on the bed facing each other. Brototi passed a pillow to her elder sister. Srabonti was about to say something, when she was disturbed by a loud shout of a street vendor trying to sell Kashmiri shawls and other handicraft items. Each year, during the winter period the streets of Kolkata would see a lot of vendors from Kashmir walking the streets and canvassing aloud to sell their products. Srabonti allowed the vendor to finish. The lazy winter afternoon filled up again with silence. She looked at Brototi and said, while continuing to chew the fennel seeds, "Why don't we start a catering business? You are such a good cook! You, me, and Hemu? What do you say?"

Brototi looked back at her with surprise.

"How can we do business we have never done it before? No one in our family has ever done it before and besides at this age?" she replied

"We can do it, let us give it a try? It will be exciting! You don't ever cry about age again! Don't you hear about start ups in the television, it will be our start up! Start up by Senior Citizens, why not! " she persuaded.

"But!" said Brototi, and then remained silent.

"Okay then you are onboard! I need to now talk to Hemu!" she concluded.

Her silence had always been taken as her consent, thought Brototi. Thirty-one years ago, her parents had asked her, after they had finalized her marriage with Soumen, if she would like to marry him. She was silent and it was taken as her consent back then as well. She had a good life with Soumen, and her consent through silence to start the catering business could also work out well, she thought. It had worked out well for her at that time, and should as well now. She felt excited at its prospect, deep in her heart. It was an opportunity to prove herself to the world. She seemed to have found a purpose in her life.

It was around 10 a.m. the following morning, Brototi's smart phone rang. "East Bengal Kitchen will be name of our catering business. Hemu is on board. We will come in the evening to your house! It is Saturday, hence we do not have to babysit!" Srabonti spoke before hanging up. Brototi was silent and her silence was again assumed her consent.

There was a different energy that evening at Brototi's house. The trio felt couple of decades younger if not more. They sat and planned in detail how they would run their business, their responsibilities, and even their marketing plan. They appeared like a bunch of youngsters brainstorming the inception of their unicorn. They had so much to do.

Brototi would take up the responsibility of cooking and managing the kitchen operations. She also managed to rope in Kundo for a few extra hours to help in the kitchen every morning. Kundo was excited at the prospect of earning some additional money. She readily said yes with a smile.

Hemu would manage the finance, collections, and delivery for now. Srabonti would take on the reigns for marketing, and receiving the calls to take the orders.

The menu was simple; three options for lunch meals: vegetarian, fish, and chicken. Each set menu option also would be served rice, lentils, crispy fried potatoes, and some tomato ginger chutney. Srabonti had forced Brototi to add the chutney, that way she would be able to have a taste of it every day.

They decided to start their operations in a week's time. Srabonti quickly jotted down the contents of the menu and designed a flier by tearing a page of the diary that Brototi was using to make notes from their meeting. Hemu and Srabonti juggled their personal responsibilities of taking care of Joy as well, yet hiding their plans from their son and daughter-in-law. Hemu organized the lunch boxes, plastic spoons, and serviettes in the next few days from Burra Bazar. He dropped them off at Brototi's house. He even managed to get two hundred stickers of East Bengal Kitchen printed in the background of red and gold. Srabonti organized a few thousand pamphlets. She had given her cell phone number on the pamphlets.

Brototi had organized the fresh produce from her selected vendors in the local market. They were very excited to hear about her starting the business. Kundo also felt proud being a member of the founding team as she walked behind Brototi through the bends of the market, carefully navigating the crowd while carrying the shopping bags.

Finally, the day arrived when their operations would start. They had mentioned in their pamphlets that they would accept calls from 9:30 a.m., and orders would be served between 12 noon and 2 p.m. The last orders can be placed till 11:45 a.m. All this was planned to manage the school pick up and drop facility for Joy. Srabonti had cooked five portions of each set menu on offer being conservative. Srabonti had also mentioned in the pamphlets specifically that operations were run by senior citizens. They all waited eagerly for the phone to ring; Srabonti for an order from a customer, Brototi to hear the confirmation of the order, Kundo to pack, and Hemu to deliver the same.

Hemu had organized an insulation bag too to keep the food warm. He had even practiced how to carry it on his motor cycle a few times by carefully observing the food delivery boys from the various mobile app companies.

It was not before 11 a.m. when Srabonti received the first call from the customer. It was a lady who called, seemed like a senior citizen. She had ordered one of each, vegetarian, fish, and chicken to try out, the first revenues for East Bengal Kitchen, a sum of Rs. 280. They were all excited. Three more orders came in before 11:40 a.m.

that made their first day of business a sellout, a revenue of Rs. 1400. They were happy, but there was a new problem that surfaced about a fortnight later as their business picked up further. There were some customers who called even at 1:30 p.m., and left voicemails sharing their disappointment. It was a good problem for their business a problem of plenty. Srabonti suggested that from 11:45 a.m. to 1 p.m. the customers could send them an SMS or WhatsApp to order, and she could confirm the order the same way. This will enable her to manage Joy while not upsetting the customers.

The plan worked well, they had now brought technology in the play. The business grew steadily and at the end of the third month, they were doing 60 – 70 meals a day. Srabonti had now employed Kundo's sister as well in the kitchen. It was becoming increasingly difficult for them to manage among the three of them. East Bengal Kitchen was becoming popular by the day and even a local community newspaper that got published on a weekly basis covered an article about them. They also received calls from a few senior citizens who wished to work with them, that too, without any remuneration. They wanted to be engaged and contribute. There were some who even were prepared to invest their money so that the initiative could grow. The trio was happy yet confused. It was something they had not anticipated three months ago. In a short space of time they had become an inspiration to a lot of senior citizens like them who were also searching for a purpose in their lives, and saw East Bengal Kitchen as a means to achieve the same.

Santanu had expressed their concern for this venture with his parents after he and his wife read about the initiative with surprise in a local community newspaper. He had even told them that he is earning enough to take care of the household expenses, there was no need for them to work hard to earn money. They both understood the underlying reason for his concern but decided not to drag the conversation and kept silent. Few days later, Sutapa received a call from Joy's school. It was from her son's teacher. She mentioned that it had been an hour since school finished and no one had come to pick up Joy. She rushed to Joy's school in anger over her in-laws. She tried calling her mother-in-law on her mobile phone from the cab but could not get through to her. She picked up Joy and reached home. Her father-in-law was seated on a sofa as she entered with Joy. She started to vent her anger on him immediately, when Srabonti entered the room after her, unlocking the door. She could hear her daughter-in-law from outside. Sutapa continued with her vent and blamed her for being irresponsible and the danger she had brought upon her grand-son.

"You are right, he is my grand-son, but he is your son, and hence your responsibility, not ours," said Srabonti while slowly sitting on the sofa next to Hemandra.

"I had done this on purpose and kept an extra packet of biscuit in Joy's school bag. I was not away I was standing on the footpath right opposite to the entrance of Joy's school. Not for a moment, I had turned my attention anywhere else. Stop taking us for granted, we have a life and as much as we love you all, you have to respect our needs and wishes. You are welcome to stay in this house as long as you can take responsibility of your son." She concluded to respond to a call on her mobile phone.

Several months had gone by since that conversation. Santanu and Sutapa still stayed with their parents, but there were some changes. Joy was picked up and dropped off by school bus. He was picked up from home but was dropped off at the offices of East Bengal Kitchen.

Yes, East Bengal kitchen had grown and had rented a small two bed room apartment as their administrative office. There were twelve senior citizens who worked there, seven women and five men. They have a team of three senior citizens who manage their logistics.

Hemu no longer had to do the delivery on his motorcycle. He now used it to take Srabonti out for a ride. Some senior citizens in the office often complained about them suddenly disappearing in the middle of the day. They had employed three young men who deliver the food on their motorcycles. The kitchen had also grown, they had renovated portion of the terrace at Brototi's house to make a bigger kitchen where eight women work. Kundo still works with them, she is now the supervisor. She no longer carried the bag and walked behind Brototi in the market. She had someone who carried the bag and walked behind her.

There was a printout that was pinned on the board at the reception of their office that read, "Grand-kids are welcome."

They also released a website and an android mobile app where customers could place their orders. Ranjan had helped them with both. He had mentioned to Brototi that he wanted to come back and be part of the venture.

The quartet of crows still come at 8 a.m. for their breakfast hosted by the fat lady. They still search for the elderly lady who used to watch them from the balcony across the narrow street, separated by the electric cables in between and fly away, without a glimpse of her.

Ammaji

Suroma lay in her bed staring at the raindrops falling on the window pane that perched quite high on the wall. She was trying to search for the blue sky amidst the cloud cover. She could not understand why she was feeling so lonely. She was not alone, being one amongst thirty others in the Dialysis Ward of a super specialty hospital. She turned her head on the pillow and saw 60 minutes still remained for the dialysis machine to finish its task. Nurses and medical attendants were moving around briskly as new set of patients substituted the old. The machines and the attendants seemed to look at each other helplessly. Business went on as usual, it seemed all inhabitants of the ward, patients, their relatives, and the medical attendants had become immune to pain. They had learned of a way to even smile back at it. It was business for the hospital and a necessity for the patients. Life for some of the inhabitants of this earth had become expensive, as they yearned to live.

Suroma turned her gaze back again towards the window, amongst the clutter of the ward. The rain had cleared suddenly leaving the clouds by themselves behind the backdrop of the blue sky. She was looking at the cloud, trying to recollect hard, the shape it had now resembled, an object or perhaps a face. It appeared like a face that seemed very familiar, yet she could not remember who it resembled. It appeared like an old wrinkled face, it was certainly not hers. It seemed to be of a woman much older than her sixty-five years. She was certain that it was a face that she had seen and met, but never had a conversation. She felt awkward and tried hard to remember, till she finally recognized the face. It was almost thirty years back, that she had last seen the face. Suroma was much younger then.

"Ammaji...," she uttered under her breath as she continued to look at the shape of the cloud minutely to confirm.

Suroma, Sujit, and Rintu, their fourteen-year-old son had just moved in to the new apartment in an upmarket South Kolkata neighbourhood. Sujit was promoted, and thus provided company accommodation. They had moved here from their modest small rented apartment in Gariahat. Suroma was very happy. She now had a much larger kitchen with cabinets on the wall. Sujit was happy as he now had a garage in the apartment block and no longer required to walk a kilometer to park his Fiat in the nearby automobile repair shop that doubled up as a parking space in the night.

The only person who was not very happy was Rintu. He was really sad to leave behind his friends and Moloyda. He had thought in his mind that he would never in his lifetime have to move from that neighbourhood. He wanted to be like his idol, Moloyda. He was not aware of what he did for a living. He seemed to be in his late twenties and was the most active member of the neighbourhood in organizing any event, religious, cultural or sports. He saw him every evening sitting and chatting with his friends on the steps of the house that belonged to the Pal's. The only thing that he liked in the new apartment was the bathroom, it was the same size as one of the bedrooms in their old rented apartment. Besides, it also had a bathtub.

The Basu's settled in quickly in their new apartment that was a located on the first floor of a three story house. Each floor had two apartments facing each other. The Agarwal's lived in the flat facing theirs on the first floor. They had been living there for a decade. They were very jovial and soon became close friends of the Basu's. They were a family of four, Mr and Mrs Agarwal, were in their late fifties, their children, son, and a daughter were in their twenties. The Agarwal's spoke Bengali as if it were their mother tongue. There was one other who lived in their apartment, Ramu, their servant. Suroma found out after two months from Mrs Agarwal that they call every servant of theirs Ramu regardless of what their name could be. She used to spend a lot of her afternoons after lunch at Mrs Agarwal's apartment, chatting and watching movies.

Since the time they moved into this apartment, Rintu had been after his father to buy them a colour television, and finally replace their black and white one. Suroma had also started to pester her husband recently on the same. She even mentioned that they should at least get a VCP[31], if not a VCR[32]. It was a matter of prestige for them. She could then invite Mrs Agarwal and her daughter for a movie and chat at her apartment as well. Sujit, evaded the relentless attacks for a few weeks, before giving in. It was a Sunday morning, when he and Rintu went to the Fancy Market in Kidderpore and bought a Sansui VCP. The colour television had arrived the previous evening and was successfully commissioned.

“If your grades go down, I will throw the television and VCP out,” Sujit said to Rintu while connecting the VCP with the television. He and Rintu had gone to Salehbhai, the owner of the local video cassette rental shop to rent couple of video cassettes. Sujit reminded Rintu that they could only rent two cassettes. There was one choice from Suroma which both Rintu and Sujit knew they could not compromise in the interest of household bliss. It was a new Bengali movie that released that year *Choto Bou*[33]. The other one was *Born Free*. Rintu had his eyes on a new Bollywood love story that was released earlier that year, where the young lovers run away from their home and

---

31 Video Cum Player

32 Video Cum Recorder

33 Youngest Daughter-in-Law

sacrifice their lives as their parents would not approve the relationship. Sujit gave him the video cassettes to hold, while he paid for the rental. He took them from his father quietly. He looked at the photo of the lion on the cover of one of the video cassettes and pondered if he really was born free?

It was one evening, when Rintu was in his small study, which was located on one corner of the long narrow balcony that ran across the two rooms of their apartment facing the driveway. The balcony was dark, the lights in it were not switched on completely. The branches of the coconut tree that stood tall on the driveway obstructed most of the light that would have entered the balcony from the apartments in front. Rintu was studying by the light of a table lamp with all his concentration when he felt as if someone had peeped into the room to check on him from behind. He thought it would certainly be his mother as always. There had been couple of occasions where she had caught him staring out of the window aimlessly, next to his study table. But he was honestly studying that evening and felt offended with the thought of not being trusted. He stood up in anger from his chair and walked up to ask his mother why she was trying to spy on him. He felt as if someone moved out of his way in the balcony to make room for him to pass through. He stopped momentarily and turned back and saw nothing.

The dim light that escaped from his study could barely reach the end of that small room. The balcony thus remained dark, he could see no one there but was certain that there was someone who had moved aside to make room for him to walk past. He saw his mother busy in the kitchen preparing dinner and in between catching glimpses of her favourite Bengali daily television soap opera. Rintu knew that his mother would never sacrifice a second of this daily soap opera to spy on him. Suroma saw him enter the dining area, the colour television was placed on one corner, the refrigerator was on the other. She was seated on a chair next to the dining table, sipping tea from her cup.

"What do you want? I had kept a bottle of water on your table. Can't you concentrate and sit and study for an hour at least without getting up? I am so worried about your future, I don't know what will happen to you if you keep getting up every half an hour like this." She complained with all her frustration, what seemed to be a fundamental right for most Bengali mothers.

Rintu was confused, he looked at her and walked back quietly to his study through the dark narrow balcony, without daring to ask her anything. He was certain somebody was spying on him as he was also about someone that moved aside to make room for him to walk past through the narrow balcony. It could not be her mother, who would it be then, he pondered.

Few days later, Sujit had to finish some urgent office work after dinner. He had laid down a few thick files on the dining table and was working from there. He was feeling tired but had no choice except to continue. Rintu and Suroma had fallen asleep. He looked at the wall clock as it struck half past eleven. He wore his reading glasses again and continued to read through the files. He would have much appreciated a cup of tea when he felt the presence of Suroma behind him. Her hands were touching the back of the chair and leaning over his shoulder to see his work.

"Will you please make me a cup of tea, it will not be before another two hours I suspect, I could hit the bed," he said without lifting his eyes. He felt little annoyed at not getting a response.

"A cup of tea please," he repeated himself as he turned to look back.

He found himself all alone. The entire house was dark except for the dining area that was illuminated by a fluorescent tube light that radiated an icy white light. He was certain there was some one behind him. He stood and walked up to his bedroom, adjusting his eyes, as he entered the dark room. He found the light switch on the left wall at the entrance and switched it on. He saw Suroma in deep sleep. There was no way she would have been able to return that quickly to her bed, besides there was no noise that he heard. He was certain of a presence. He left the light on as he went back to the dining area. He felt bit anxious. He quickly switched off the lights in the dining area and walked back briskly towards his bed room. He briefly stopped by Rintu's room and momentarily switched on the lights to check on him before he retired for the night. Soon, he was fast asleep. He left door of Rintu's room open intentionally as he did theirs, switched off the light and paced up in the darkness to take his place next to Suroma.

As he lay next her with his face towards the wall, away from her, he was certain that someone was standing at the doorway waiting for him to fall asleep. The ceiling fan was rotating at its maximum speed, it was not warm at all that July night as it rained incessantly outside. He sweated, yet he slid inside the bed sheet that Suroma had covered herself with. He did not mention anything to Suroma next morning. He did not even respond to her, when she complained about him leaving his files scattered on the table the previous night.

Life went on in the Basu household, though occasionally, Sujit and Rintu could feel the presence of someone, overlooking them. Neither Sujit nor Rintu spoke about their experiences with the other or together with Suroma. It was a hot October afternoon, Suroma was alone in the apartment. She had just finished eating her lunch and was in her kitchen to prepare a special meal for dinner. It was Sujit's birthday and he had requested for the spicy mutton curry with big round potatoes. He had even got up early that morning, stood in the queue and got the best part of the goat from the neighbourhood butcher. She had added dhokar[34] dalna and tomato chutney with khejur[35] from her side in the menu. She wanted to finish her work to allow her enough time to relax and watch television in the evening. She would need to cook only some rice in the evening then.

She was in complete control of her kitchen, multi-tasking in harmony. It appeared as if she was the conductor of an orchestra and every object in the kitchen was her musicians, playing in harmony, each waiting for their respective turn. She had the pressure cooker on one of her two burner gas stove, where the mutton was being cooked and lentil cakes or dhoka being fried on the other. The pressure cooker whistled for the second time announcing that the mutton curry had been cooked. The chef now turned off the burner and went back to finishing the tomato chutney. She tasted few drops of it from the palm of her hand and felt something is missing. She opened the cabinet doors in the kitchen over the gas burner and was searching for something. She heard a voice from behind that seemed to be of an elderly woman asking her to search for raisins in next cabinet.

"Right," Suroma said spontaneously, laughing at herself and then quickly realizing that she was talking to

---

34 Lentil cake curry – speciality Bengali dish

35 Dates

herself. She was however certain she heard a voice. She quickly turned around, keeping the plastic bag full of raisins on the kitchen top. She distinctly saw a shadow disappear quickly into Rintu's room which opened into the long balcony from the other end of the room. She was scared, she quickly turned off the gas stove and snatched the house keys from the key holder on the walls and rushed out of the apartment, shutting the door aloud behind her. She was very anxious, scared, and was looking back at the door of her apartment while relentlessly pressing on the calling bell of the Agarwal's. She seemed to be losing patience in the thirty seconds it took for Ramu to open the door. In her anxiety, she did not realise that, the door was now open, but she was still looking back at her apartment as she continued to press on the calling bell. She was convinced that somebody was looking at her from behind the closed door of her apartment through the eye hole. It appeared like a dilating pupil of an elderly eye. Mrs Agarwal was now standing behind Ramu, close to the doorway.

"What happened? Come in please, you look scared, all well?"she asked while walking back into her drawing room with Suroma following her. She sat on the sofa facing Suroma, allowing bit of time for her tall and obese structure to settle down. She seemed to have for some reason suspected from the look on Suroma's face, the cause of her anxiety. She asked Ramu to bring them some water. Suroma was still in a state of shock. Ramu brought them water and closed the door behind him.

“There is someone in my apartment, do not know who, but someone for sure, I saw a shadow. Someone was watching me from behind while I was in my kitchen. I will stay here till Rintu comes from school, can’t be back there alone,” she stuttered with long pauses sipping water in between.

Mrs Agarwal looked at her with equanimity. “It could be her,” she continued.

“Who?” Surama asked still scared.

“Ammaji!”

She told Surama that their apartment was vacant for little more than three years before they moved in it. A Punjabi family lived there before them. They were a family of four, husband, wife, their teenage daughter, and Ammaji, Mr Arora’s mother. She knew the family well. They were all so busy in their own respective worlds, that no one had time for Ammaji. They fed her, gave her clothes, but did not seem to give her much of their time. Ammaji shared a room with her grand-daughter. She was neglected and lonely amongst her own. She was mostly by herself all day, alone in the house. Her son and daughter–in–law were in office, and her grand-daughter in school. Mrs Agarwal would often see her standing in the balcony all alone, looking out on the road, watching the birds as they sat on the branches of the coconut tree that leaned on the balcony.

"I don't think she means any harm to you," Mrs Agarwal finished looking at Suroma, who was listening engrossed, feeling sorry for the old woman. She stood while in her thoughts about Ammaji, the fear in her seemed to have been replaced with empathy. She went back to her apartment, declining the offer and insistence of her host to stay back for some more time.

She opened the door of her apartment and walked in as the door shut behind her. She looked straight down the passage that led to the bed rooms, Rintu's was on the right, theirs straight ahead. "Ammaji," Suroma addressed to the silence of the apartment. She noticed a shadow stop in stillness, at the entrance of Rintu's room. The calling bell rang in quick succession. She opened the door with a delay, collecting her thoughts back, Rintu walked in.

They sat down together as a family for dinner that evening. Suroma had also made rice pudding on occasion of Sujit's birthday. She felt satisfied to see Sujit and Rintu taking second help of the mutton curry. They chatted and laughed as a family. Suroma was seated on a chair facing the entrance of Rintu's room, diagonally. In a moment of laughter, her eyes met those of an old woman standing at the entrance of Rintu's room, overlooking Sujit. She had kept her left hand gently on the frame of the door and was looking at them. She could see her distinctly, a short stocky old woman in a white salwar suit. She smiled at her in respect, acknowledging her presence.

Rintu had once brought up over dinner that he felt there was a ghost in the apartment, Sujit also shared his experiences but Suroma had dismissed their view, with a smile telling them that it was a figment of their imagination. Since that incident, she had spent more of her afternoons in her apartment than visiting Mrs Agarwal.

Ammaji lived with the Basu's for the next three years till Sujit got promoted again and they moved to a bigger apartment in New Alipore.

Suroma thought as the nurse slowly removed the needles from her arm, would Ammaji still be present in that apartment. She imagined Ammaji walking around in an empty apartment in loneliness, from one room to other. It would be dark, the sounds of her feet as she dragged them slowly and carefully, tearing the silence, echoed in Suroma's mind.

Sujit was standing next to her bed in the hospital. He had also grown older. Rintu had settled in USA, it was only them now in their apartment. She was also lonely. She looked up through the glass to see the clouds clearing away. She walked slowly with Sujit through the busy corridors of the hospital. He was holding her hand as they stood in front of the elevator, waiting for it to arrive.

List

"You will never be able to say it," spoke Rubaina. The words from her mouth seemed like a sharp pair of scissors, cutting meticulously through the silence of the lazy Belconnen afternoon. The perfect spring afternoon appeared quite disdain to her as she watched Raj trying to pack his bag. As always, it was a mess, he had spread all his clothes on the sofa and the chairs of their drawing room. Rubaina had now stopped even trying to convince Raj of a more structured method to pack his bags. She had made several attempts in the two years that they lived together.

"Don't you worry my love, I have rehearsed it to perfection this time," said Raj, as he turned around towards Rubaina. She was sitting on the sofa behind him making space among the heap of clothes that Raj had dumped on it. Rubaina looked at him, taking her eyes momentarily off the novel she was reading.

Her eyes met Raj's as she nodded her head in disagreement.

"You don't believe me, hear me out," he replied turning himself towards her. Rubaina ignored him, turning another page of the novel.

"Ma, I love Rubaina and I want to... I want to…" he stuttered and struggled. His eyes seemed to request hers for help. She did not even lift her eyes. A storm seemed to be growing inside her and then she let go.

"You will never, you will never ever be able to tell your mother that you want to marry me." There was more pain than anger in her voice. She wanted to leave the room, when Raj held her hands.

"I will say it this time, I will," he said, turning her with a slight force towards him, locking his eyes in hers.

"Your hesitation is because, I am..." she paused.

"Muslim," Raj completed. He placed the palm of his hands on her cheeks as he nodded his head denying.

"It's been three years," she said. Her eyes became moist with tear drops perched on the edge.

"Believe me this one last time please."

She looked up at him while surrendering to his tight embrace. It reminded her of the first time she had noticed him in the Accounting class of their MBA course on a cold winter evening in Canberra. There was something in him that she could not stop falling for. There was also something in her that he could not escape from either. They were different, yet similar. They had a lot in common, speaking the same mother tongue, roots in a geography which was dissected into two different countries by a line that cut through enough hearts, as it grouped people by religion. The Hindu dominated Western part of Bengal and the Muslim dominated Eastern part. They spoke Bangla, though they understood each other, their accents and choice of words were different to mean the same thing.

Rubaina Ahmed was three years old when her parents had migrated to Australia from Dhaka. It was during the mid-eighties. She had been back twice since to the country of her birth. The first time when she was ten, and the next when she had turned eighteen. She could not relate with her relatives both times and had always counted days to return back to her home. She spoke their language but probably could not think in it.

Rubaina was an independent, intelligent, beautiful, and an expressive woman. She was what her parents always dreamt her to be. Her parents worked hard as immigrants to raise her and also to build their restaurant business. Her father had always wanted her to be a corporate woman. He had always thought of his daughter, every time he saw a corporate woman in his restaurant. She had fulfilled his dream. She had graduated in Accounting and was working for a global consulting company. He was proud of her.

It was a cold July evening when Rubaina Ahmed had first interacted with Raj Chakraborty. They had first spoken during the middle of an accounting class, when Raj who was seated in the row just behind her in the huge classroom which was like an auditorium. He had accidently dropped his pen and the same had rolled on to stop at Rubaina's feet.

"My pen, next to your feet," were the first words that Raj had whispered from behind. She had felt his warm breath, falling on the back of her neck. She probably would not have felt it had she not tied her hair up with a clip that day. She had picked it up and held it in her hand looking ahead, when Raj had picked it up from her fingers.

"Thanks," he had said, while she had not bothered to respond. They first saw each other 30 minutes after that incident. The lectures finished and they had walked down the stairs of the auditorium. He desperately wanted to see the face that helped him. She was wearing a red cardigan, her long black hair was guarding her face as he struggled to see it from the side. She had a black overcoat in her hand. A crowd of students had now come between them. His heart was beating fast and he had no explanation of why he felt restless to see her face. He was making all the attempts to make the next contact of purpose, even pushing himself through the crowd to the annoyance of a few students to keep close behind her. She had noticed it.

"Hi, I am Raj Chakraborty, thank you for picking up my pen," he hurriedly said to her, just as they were to go past the doorway of the auditorium. His accent, especially when he said Chakraborty, had Bengali written all over.

"Bengali?" she asked with a smile, stepping aside towards the hallway. Raj nodded positively without being able to take his eyes off her. He wanted time to freeze and listen to the silence of his soul. There was an awkward silence for ten seconds.

"Rubaina," she said breaking the silence, introducing herself. They kept meeting, but not outside the Accounting lecture. It was not until two more months, as spring ushered in that Raj asked Rubaina out. Well, actually he started the sentence and stuttered till Rubaina completed, "You are asking me out for a date?"

They had spent the day at the local flower show. They spoke, laughed, and walked amidst the tulips and the roses, as love blossomed. Rubaina noticed his smile, he was caring and shy. She was falling for him while he had already fallen. Raj Chakraborty, a boy from a staunch Brahmin Hindu family in South Kolkata fell in love with Rubaina Ahmed.

It was towards the end of the final semester of their course that they had decided to live together. Rubaina had suggested it to Raj. She had moved out from her parents' home towards the beginning of the semester. Her parents had objected initially, but soon realized that it was normal in their adopted country.

Rubaina had told her parents about Raj, when he had moved in to stay with her. It was more about informing them than seeking their permission. She had once invited Raj at her parents' house in Florey for dinner. It was about a week before he moved in to her apartment. Raj enjoyed the Bengali dishes that Rubaina's mother had prepared, especially the Hilsa[36] with mustard sauce. Her parents had approved of Raj, at least he spoke the same language that acted as a bridge to connect their two religions.

Raj, on the other hand, had not informed his parents. He had fought the battle within him and with Rubaina ever since. He had a feeling his parents will never be able to come to terms with their son living together with a Muslim girl with roots in Bangladesh. They would certainly disown him. He had often heard stories from both his parents on how they had to leave everything in erstwhile Bangladesh to come to the Western part of Bengal and start their lives all over again. They had lost everything to the riots, seen the religious violence, Muslims oppress the Hindus. They could never let go of those memories. He was scared to lose them as well as Rubaina, and thus, chose silence and denial. He had always wanted to escape the reality, but that was not to be.

"I will tell them, but that is not what I am worried about, I am more worried when..." he continued as he held her in an embrace.

---

36 Fresh water fish

"When... What?" Rubaina asked as she freed herself. She sat on the sofa and tied her hair in a knot. Raj came and sat on the floor in front of her, keeping the bag he was packing aside.

"See, there is no doubt that we will get married soon, but the worry is after that, we need to adjust with each other's parents when they come to visit us or we visit them."

She looked at him confused. He continued in exuberance, "This is where we have to be careful of using the right terminology, so that they are at ease."

"What?"

"We need to make a list, quick get pen and paper, forget it, let's use your phone," he continued giving Rubaina her phone that lay on the sofa next to her. Rubaina looked at him in dismay, while he kept going unfazed.

"Let's first make a list of the words we need to use when my parents come to live with us, and then we can make the list that we will use for your parents. No, actually we would need only one list, follow one column for my parents and the next for your parents." He spoke in exuberance, without checking Rubaina's reaction. She wanted to say something but Raj continued.

"Ready? Okay, let's type. Make three columns, headings will be English, Hindu – Bangla; Muslim – Bangla. Now for the words and please free to add in…

Father – Baba – Abba

Mother – Ma – Ammi

Water – Jol – Paani

Mutton – Mangsho – Gosht

Bath – Snan – Goshul

Greetings – Nomoshkar – Salaam..."

He wanted to continue when Rubaina interrupted him, "Why are you doing this?" She kept her phone on the sofa next to her and held his face with her palms.

"I know you love me very much, probably much more than I love you. You don't need to do this Raj. We did not fall in love with each other for a reason. We just fell in love, without thinking about our religion or where we came from, or if anybody would approve of it. So why do we have to sell so hard of a decision that we own. I really don't care if your parents approve of our marriage, all I know is that I love you and we love each other and that is all that matters."

She rested her head on his chest, he put his arms around her waist. She heard his heart beat. They appeared like two sequoia trees, separate yet united by their roots that spread over each other.

Raj's mobile phone rang breaking the silence in the room. It was his mother. Raj took the phone as Rubaina got up to the leave the room. She stopped in the short hallway leading to their bedroom, when she heard Raj speak on the phone.

"Ma, I love Rubaina, we have been living together for the last three years. She is a very nice girl, although she is Muslim, I know you will like her. I want to marry her. I will talk to you and Baba in detail when I meet you tomorrow. Keep well." He said spontaneously, unfazed without inhibition and un-rehearsed. He felt light from within. A stone lifted from his chest. He turned in disbelief, searching for Rubaina as he finished his call.

He saw her hand coming out from the hallway, he held it, pulled her towards him, and then slowly kept his palms on the side of her face. There was silence as tears appeared in the corner of his eyes.

"I said it Rubaina, I said it." His voice choked. They were in the hallway, a different one to where Rubaina first spoke with him. They stood there holding each other in a new found hope filled with strength.

Love had deleted the list.

MCC

Mahadev Pal had never felt more helpless than before the eve of his twenty-fifth work anniversary at the Global Multi-national Software Company, where he worked. He was among the five hundred chosen ones who were given the option to retire voluntarily. He was offered the Voluntary Retirement Scheme (VRS). There was nothing voluntary about the offer. He had been amongst the dedicated and faithful employees that served the company, and yet he was among the chosen ones. He read the mail from HR few times over that evening, sitting in his office cubicle in disbelief. He had never ever committed any of the corporate cardinal sins. He had never said no to anything his manager and the company had ever asked of him. He had worked hard to get to the level of a Director in that company. This was certainly no ordinary feat to achieve.

He had always worked late, but that evening he was waiting patiently for his manager to return to his cabin. It was 9 p.m. and his wife had already called him thrice to inquire when he would come home. He had not picked up her call and sent her a message that read: "In a conference call, will be late, u eat and sleep." He knew SRC, Sadashiv Roy Chowdhury was in a call with a customer from United Kingdom. He was in the conference room towards the end of the corridor. He had checked SRC's cabin twice and was relieved to see his laptop and car keys on the table through the transparent glass walls. He waited like a predator for an opportunity to speak with SRC, while he was the prey.

Finally, the moment that he was waiting for so long came. He noticed SRC going past his cubicle and enter his office. In a flash, he picked up his notebook and pen and headed straight towards his boss's cabin.

"Sir how can this happen?" he exclaimed with disappointment.

"Let's talk about it tomorrow."

"Sir, please I have given everything to the company, why me?" he appealed.

"I understand, but you are not alone. But it does not allow you to send me five messages in a space of forty five minutes that read: "Urgent need to meet." You must understand I have other priorities to deal with, than to discuss your VRS." SRC responded in an offended tone.

Mahadev Pal felt the pain he had never expected this especially from a man to whom he had never said no. He had even missed his son's fifteenth birthday last year and travelled to Chicago for a day, to absorb curses of an unhappy customer. He had spent more time in air than in

Chicago. He left the room as the glass door closed behind him. He did not look back, went to his cubicle, packed his belongings and walked towards the elevator. The descent from the sixth floor felt longer than ever before. He took it as his failure. The streets of Sector V in Salt Lake, Kolkata were still not that deserted. He hailed at a yellow cab that was not air-conditioned, and jumped into it.

He could not stop thinking about the evening as he unlocked and the opened the door of his flat carefully to enter. His wife and son were asleep. He cautiously opened the door of his son's room and found him asleep. The moonlight that entered the room through the window fell on his face. He went in and pulled the curtain to block it from Tublu's face. He changed and quietly slipped into the bed next to Mohua. He tossed and turned and could not sleep, which disturbed Mohua. She grumbled and he finally lay stationary on his back looking at the ceiling fan as it rotated above him. He thought repeatedly how his name could be in that list in spite of him following the ten commandments of a good loyal corporate citizen. He was taught them by one his earlier bosses when he had just joined the company. Two decades and a bit had passed since that day, but he could never forget them. They were, as he said to himself to check if he had missed out on any before giving in to sleep on the tenth commandment.

1. *Never say no to your boss*
2. *Commitment means working over weekends*

3. Sacrifice personal needs for corporate responsibilities

4. Rules will always over ride principles

5. Diplomacy is the differentiator

6. Being Non-Committal will save you

7. Cage your free spirit

8. Find the shoulder that can take the load

9. Set up conference calls to communicate anything and everything.

10. Emails are saviours, never fail to send one at the slightest opportunity.

Krutika Parekh, the HR Manager arrived half an hour late for her meeting with Mahadev, the next morning. She had recently joined the Kolkata office from Mumbai. Mahadev had heard about an attractive, petite, and single young lady joining the HR team, but never imagined for once that he would be required to meet her under such circumstances. Krutika apologized unconditionally as she greeted Mahadev with a smile. They sat in her office, surrounded by transparent glass walls on three sides and an uncomfortable silence within. He did not want to retire, at least not then. He felt that it was incredibly unfair to have the last nail on his corporate coffers to be hammered by such beautiful hands. Krutika broke the silence.

"You have worked so hard for the company, MP, sorry feels bit awkward to call you Mahadev as I am staunch follower of Lord Mahadev[37]. Is it okay if I call you MP?" He nodded in obedience. He was used to it. Krutika continued further with ease.

"I am sure you are so looking forward to your retired life. I have heard how committed you were, working weekends, personal sacrifices, 14-16 hour days. They say you are an inspiration. This means you have already served the company much more than the hours that were required of you, had you worked till the age of sixty. This is efficiency. I am so glad you decided to take up the VRS. I am sure your family would be so looking forward to spending more time with you. Here, you need to sign on all these pages where you see a cross marked."

Mahadev looked at her mesmerized in silence and then finally broke his silence.

"I do not want to retire."

Krutika smiled and responded, "You are among the few chosen ones, take this as a benefit. You know time is the real currency for life. You will now have all the time for yourself, your family; you will have your weekends back, think of it. You have such a lot of experience, why don't you think of starting a consultancy of your own. You can work much lesser hours to make much more money on your own terms going forward."

37 Hindu deity

"But..." Mahadev raised a short revolt as Krutika lent him a pen.

"Here the pen, please sign I need to close your case, am already late for my next meeting." Krutika finished. He was obedient again.

Mahadev signed on all the papers. He had begun to read each and every page as he used to read the Statements of Work from his customers. Krutika asked him to hurry up and mentioned that these are standard clauses and were non-negotiable. She was stern this time, yet not forgetting to smile. She reminded Mahadev, just as he was about to leave her office to return all the company assets to one of her team members before he left for the day.

"The company would not like to bother you from tomorrow, in fact you are welcome to leave now as well if you would like," she said as Mahadev stood to leave.

The Sun thus set on the corporate career of Mahadev Pal that day. He sent a good bye mail to all mentioning his personal email address. He waited for another half an hour in front of his mail box and only saw three responses. There were from two Delivery Managers who had responded to the SRC's inquiry. One of the Delivery Managers had responded saying, "No Knowledge Transition required, all good," and the other responded with "Same here." He returned the laptop and his identity card and left the building empty handed. He saw a bunch of young professionals, probably new recruits waiting at the reception. It was just after 2 p.m. when he exited the company facilities where he had once joined as a new recruit. Nobody remembered to congratulate him as left the company premise that afternoon on his twenty-fifth work anniversary. Business went around him as usual.

Mahadev enjoyed the warm air that hit his face sitting by the window of the yellow ambassador taxi. Krutika's advice kept resonating on him. He took the decision after some deliberation with himself. He decided to heed on her advice and start his own consulting company. He did not feel worried for some reason, on the contrary, he felt light and enjoyed the new found freedom. The first thing he reminded himself was to delete the office email application from his phone. He felt like running on the busy Eastern Bypass motorway while shouting aloud 'Holiday', much like the character of a king who had run in excitement shouting 'Chuti chuti!', which meant holiday in Bengali, in a famous Bengali film that he had seen as a child.

Mohua was surprised when Mahadev walked in that afternoon through the front door. She had never seen Mahadev come home ever from work while the sun was bright and shining in the twenty years of her married life. She was even surprised to see him enter without his laptop bag.

"What happened? Are you alright?" she asked.

He asked her for a glass of water as he sank into the black leather sofa in the drawing room. He started narrating the incidents as his wife went to fetch him a glass of water. He paused to drink the water and continued. He shared everything with her except for his views on Krutika.

"Voluntary retirement!" exhaled Mohua and continued "Now what? You will be at home all day?" She had got used to her independence for the day and was worried now of losing it. She had almost a whole a day for herself at least till 4:30 p.m. or 5 p.m. till her son returned from school finishing couple of his tuitions. She was also worried about the control over the remote of her television set during the day.

He told Mohua that he will start a consultancy company called MCC. She looked at him in surprise, her mouth wide open like the entrance of a dark cave.

"MCC!" she exclaimed.

"Yes. Mahadev Corporate Coaching, MCC! I will teach my Ten Commandments for corporate success to the final year graduating students. This will make them hot cakes for recruitment. They will be productive from day one!"

"Are you sure? I mean, will you be able to run your own business? No one in your family has ever been in business before," Mohua asked cynically.

"I am in festive mood; no amount of your scepticism will dampen my spirits. Pack your bags, we are going for a short vacation to Darjeeling for a week, day after tomorrow."

"Are you in your senses? Tublu will miss his tuitions, he is writing his grade ten exams this year," Mohua exclaimed

"It's his summer vacation it has been over five years that we had last gone on a vacation together. It will do no harm to your son. Let him relax a bit," Mahadev replied as he saw Mohua frown sitting next to him on the sofa.

"Please…" he continued holding her hand locking his eyes in her's.

Mahadev booked the air tickets to Bagdogra airport, transport to Darjeeling, and hotel online before Tublu came home. He had requested Mohua not to tell anything to Tublu as he wanted to disclose the news of this vacation to him.

Tublu could not believe his ears when Mahadev disclosed the news of their vacation to Darjeeling over dinner.

"Are you alright Baba? What about your work?" he had responded, to which Mahadev smiled back.

Mahadev had not enjoyed his morning cup of tea more in many years. It was a beautiful morning, sun was out and they could see the Kanchenjunga ranges on the horizon. Tublu was looking at them as he ate his omelette in between. Mohua sat in-front observing the men in her life. She too had not felt happier in the many mornings before that.

Mahadev heard a male voice calling out his name from behind in Bengali as he stood in the queue of the buffet breakfast to refill his plate. The accent seemed like a non-Bengali speaking. He turned around and saw a fat man with a pale complexion about his age smiling at him.

"Kishorilal Agarwal!" Mahadev exclaimed.

Kishorilal or Kishori as Mahadev called him many years back, had dropped out of college after their first year together. He had joined his father's trading business in Burrabazar in central Kolkata. Mahadev had not met him after that. Kishori and Mahadev have both changed since then, except they still remained clean shaven. Kishori had a put on a lot of weight with a hairline that had receded to the point where hair only around the periphery of his head could be observed. Mahadev recognized him from his smile and the mole below his left eye.

Mahadev waited for Kishori to finish plating up his breakfast as Mohua watched them.

"Been a very long time, how are you doing Mahadev?" Kishori asked as he walked up.

"All good! You?"

"Good! Business is good," Kishori replied and then continued with his characteristic smile, "I saw you when I entered the breakfast area but was not very sure until I looked at you more carefully in the queue. Then I thought let me give a shout, if it is a mistake then I will just say sorry."

"Come join us? You are with your family?"

"No, no, I am by myself for a business meeting. I am also opening another engineering college near Siliguri. Let's meet around 4 p.m. for tea. I have a dinner meeting and then going back to Kolkata tomorrow morning."

Kishori excused himself as Mahadev observed him join a group of men on the far end of the breakfast area.

Mahadev and Kishori met later in that afternoon. Mahadev shared everything about his life since the time they had separated till his vision of Mahadev Coaching Centre, MCC.

"Brilliant!" Kishori exclaimed and then continued. "You are an international figure, why don't you offer your services to my engineering colleges. You can work with the final year engineering students and my placement cell."

Mahadev was a bit surprised. He did remember Kishori mention about him opening an engineering college near Siliguri, but did not ever imagine him to build such a fortune in the higher education industry as a drop out.

"Sunrise Engineering College!" Kishore chuckled interrupting Mahadev's thoughts and then spoke further. "You have not heard of the Sunrise Colleges? That is mine. You have to help me, this is the gap I feel now why our placement is weak. I will call my principal and ask him to meet you at the earliest."

Mahadev could not believe his luck as he saw Kishori call the principle of his Baruipur campus and talk to him about MCC.

Luck often requires initiatives to be taken before it can act.

It has since been three years, Mahadev and MCC never looked back. Mahadev has now tied up with nine private engineering institutes in two states in Eastern India. His students have now become hot properties for large multi-nationals to recruit. They are treated as the perfect recipe that every corporate wants to have a slice of. He even has a popular Youtube channel. The most satisfying experience for him in recent years was that of being invited to offer training to the new recruits by the company where he was blessed to get a voluntary retirement package.

He has now even employed Mohua. She still watches the Bengali soap opera, but in moderation. She is his training coordinator. Tublu their son is in the first year of Engineering, studying in a University in Mangalore. They spend all the time with each other, work and personal.

Sometimes the best opportunities present themselves in the middle of an adversary. They had never been happier.

And That Day

Raj unlocked the door of his apartment and stepped inside. He had his eyes on Priya, who leaned on the wall uncomfortably next to the doorway. He quickly switched on the lights and helped Priya in, and assisted her to sit on a chair next to the dining table. He kept his laptop bag on the dining table and realized that the door was still open. Mrs Ghosh, his neighbour opened the door of her apartment timing it to perfection as Raj reached back at his doorway. She looked at him, over her spectacles. She looked at him suspiciously as he carefully smiled back at her in acknowledgement before closing the door, while she continued to stare. She had not reacted to his smile. He quickly checked through the eye hole of his door and found her still standing in front of her door for a few more seconds, as she nodded her head in disbelief making assumptions probably that were best not thought. He did not blame her much. She had never seen any young women visiting him ever. There have only been two women who had ever entered that apartment since he took it on rent, couple of years back. They were Padma, his maid, and his mother, who would visit him couple of times a year.

He quickly turned his attention towards Priya and poured her a glass of water.

“Here, are you feeling better?” he asked with concern placing the glass carefully on a coaster on the dining table in front of her.

“Much better. I don’t how what happened, I suddenly felt a bit giddy and fell...” she said as Raj interrupted her with a smile to complete her sentence

“To half open your eyes to see me.”

“Coffee?” he enquired further.

She nodded her head affirmatively and looked around the room.

The room did not have too many furniture. A small square glass top dining table with four chairs of which she had occupied one, 42 inch flat screen television mounted on the wall diagonally opposite to where she sat. The set up box was balanced carefully on top of the television and the gap between the top edge of the television and the wall. The remote control lay on top of it. There was a mattress in front of the television, pushed up to the wall. There were two pillows, each with a different pillow cases. A bedsheet covered the mattress very loosely and was coming out from all corners exposing the mattress underneath. It did not match either of the pillow cases. There were some business magazines and some loose sheets of paper that appeared to be print outs of some project report scattered over the bedsheet.

She liked the view through huge sliding window that opened out on the other side of the room. It was well secured with iron grills on the ninth floor as it overlooked the suburb of Golf Green[38] and the glitter of the city lights—a proof of ever expanding city of Kolkata.

"You have a great tidy place in here!" she called out to Raj who was in the kitchen.

"Yes, almost, needs to be organized a bit," he responded trying to pour the boiling milk, diluted with water in equal proportion into the coffee mugs.

"You still in Bangalore?" he asked while coming out of the kitchen balancing a tray that had two mugs of coffee.

"Yes, same job from campus," she replied.

"2 sugars, half and half, milk and water, right?" He said, putting the tray on the dining table.

"You have not forgotten much I see!"

"Nice!" she certified sipping the coffee and continued, "your wife will have no problems at all with you, sorry married?"

"No, but what happened with you, I was quite surprised to find you lying there in the middle of the crowd, around the corner of my apartment. I would never approach a

38 Suburb of Kolkata

crowd like that, not sure what happened today. You are lucky. Did you check your belongings in your bag, purse and mobile phone?" He said with concern as he sipped his coffee at the end of it.

"How long has it been since we last met?" Priya asked trying to change the topic.

"Three years," he replied, only to continue, "Priya, if you were not feeling well you should not have not left home, this is Kolkata and not..."

"You have not changed a wee bit Raj Mitra, Mr. Dependable of our college" she intervened not allowing Raj to finish.

"So what brings you to Kolkata and more so, to my side of the town?"

"Office work, in fact I came this side of the town to meet someone and was going back towards New Town, where I am staying in my company guest house," she replied finishing her coffee and keeping the mug back on the tray.

"How is Rohan?" Raj inquired.

Raj could see Priya feeling uncomfortable. She felt ill. She covered her mouth with her left palm and barely could ask Raj directions to the toilet. as he quickly pointed towards them.

She rushed in. Raj could hear her from outside making attempts to vomit, then there was silence as she stepped out wiping her face with a towel. Raj took it from her and helped her sit down.

"You, all right? Do you want me to take you to a Doctor? We have a clinic next door, they will be open now," he asked Priya, quickly looking at his wrist watch.

She sat down on the chair next to the dining table, poured some water for herself from the bottle that Raj had kept earlier.

"Not required. I am fine, it happens sometimes in this condition," she replied with a pause after drinking a gulp of water.

"I am pregnant," Priya continued looking at Raj, who now sat across her on the dining table. "It's the third month."

"Congratulations!" he responded softly trying to smile.

"We were to get married in three weeks. Me and Rohan." She said poignantly, as Raj looked at her in dismay.

"Were to? What do you mean?" he asked as his thoughts took him four years back when they studied together in the college. The days and times were different. It was a year before they completed their graduation, Raj,

Rohan, and Priya. They were friends, but it was Raj who had fallen for Priya before Rohan.

Raj had nothing exceptional about him. He was a boy next door, average looking and an above average student. Sometimes the world does not have the time to evaluate what laid beneath the sheath. The shortlists are made mostly on the basis of external positioning. The only thing that was exceptional about him was his love for Priya, which he had never expressed.

Priya Pillai was the perfect combination of beauty and brains. She was slightly dusky in complexion, slender with an average height. She was visible everywhere from Reading Library to Dramatics club to coffee shops. She had a smile that boys could do anything to have a glimpse of. There was an air of confidence in her demeanour, yet being quite approachable.

Rohan was the overconfident, good looking tall lad from a rich family from Tollygunge in Kolkata. He had a gift of the gab, but Raj was a better student than him and helped Priya a lot with her studies. Rohan had a bike and a carefree attitude. Raj did not possess either.

Raj and Priya were good friends and could talk with ease on anything right from sex to sociology with each other. Priya took him as her confidante, yet he could never express himself. The fear of rejection always got better of him.

He had only shared his love for Priya with Pradip. Pradip had always encouraged him to tell her. He never could. He was worried if she rejected his love and never met or spoke with him ever, after that.

He could never understand how Priya fell for Rohan when it was she, who had asked him to tell Rohan not to bother her. He did, and then there was a break in the college for couple weeks before they got back for the final semester. He came back to see Rohan and Priya going around. She had fallen for him. He had later heard from Pradip, who stayed back in the campus during the break that, Priya and Rohan had also stayed back. Something happened during the break and Rohan walked into her life.

Raj had never asked her anything and had slowly withdrawn himself. Priya did not clarify anything either. It was around that time Pradip had introduced him with an old monk, which reduced his pain temporarily but not completely.

"Rohan must have run away refusing to marry her and take responsibility of the baby to be born, he had feared this. He knew this is where there relationship would end up, in fact he never thought it will get this far." He told himself as Priya replied, as if in response to his thought.

"Rohan is dead."

The room was filled with an awkward silence. Raj felt guilty for this thoughts.

"I am sorry, how did it happen?" he asked softly breaking the silence in the room.

"Motor bike accident. He went to Goa with some of his friends to enjoy the last few days of his independence before our marriage. They all had a bit too much to drink. He lost control of his bike and it skidded. Ashok, who was his pillion survived with serious injuries, but Rohan did not. He skidded straight into a milestone by the side of the road," she said with numbness.

"When did this happen?" Raj uttered.

"A month back," Priya replied as she rose from the chair and slowly walked up to stand by the window. She enjoyed the cool night breeze touching her face. She closed her eyes and stood there for a moment.

Raj watched her as he rolled his fingers on the edges of the coffee mug.

"I wish I could have told him before he left for Goa that he was to become a father. I wanted to surprise him on his return. He would have at least been aware of his new responsibility and perhaps been more careful." She spoke looking at the darkness outside, beneath, the city lights glittered.

"What will you do now, I mean..." Raj stuttered.

"With the baby?" she quickly replied turning towards Raj.

"You know this was the exact question, his mother also asked me?" Priya continued as she walked up and sat on the chair next to Raj by the dining table.

"She stays not far from here. She was not aware till earlier this evening about my pregnancy. I had gone to meet her to inform her." She said looking straight at Raj. There was an answer in her eyes that Raj read.

"It's not that easy," he replied slowly trying to look away to avoid an eye contact.

She was quiet for a while and then spoke.

"She said the same thing as well, and I told her that I had come to inform her as it is important for her to know I was carrying Rohan's child. I could read a worry in her eyes, about how the society may take to this news."

"How about your parents?" Raj asked poignantly.

"It is my decision. I am not seeking permission from the world." She replied indifferently.

"Better said than done, Priya, you are taking a wrong decision again," Raj retorted impulsively. He realized as soon he uttered the words. He had hid his emotions from the world, except for Pradip for such long time, but why could he not then.

"Again?" Priya asked with a surprise and then exhaled softly looking at Raj, as he slowly looked away.

"Raj!"

"I would have told you, couldn't you have waited for couple of weeks, I would have told you!" He did not make any attempt to control himself now. He felt as if it was his last chance.

"Is that why you distanced yourself from us during the last semester?" she asked.

The room was again filled up with an awkward silence as they sat amidst it.

"It's late and I must leave," Priya spoke. She picked up her black handbag that slung from the edge of a chair.

Raj remained seated, his attention focused on the coffee mug that he was holding on to tightly in his palms. He could see a blurred image of Priya walk past him towards the door that stood behind him.

"Marry me," he said as he heard the door open and then close quickly behind him. He was not sure if she had heard him. He felt like running after her. He realized that they had not even exchanged their mobile numbers. She would still be waiting for the elevator to arrive on the tenth floor, but he could not move.

"Good luck! Good luck Priya..." he whispered as he saw a drop of tear fall into the coffee mug that he was looking into.

Superstar Struggler

He stood by wings adjusting the microphone that was clipped on to his blue shirt, between the second and third button from the top. He nervously waited for his name to be called out by the announcer. He had been on stage and faced the lights numerous times before, but it was different, that day. He was invited by a college in Bhowanipur, Kolkata to deliver a talk on his life.

"Friends, please join me in welcoming on stage, Mithoon Khan," a young man announced. Mithoon Khan walked on to the stage, waving to the crowd in response to their loud applause. He stood in the middle of the stage. His heart was beating faster than ever before. He was also feeling good, and pinched his left wrist mildly to ensure it was not a dream. He had dreamt of that very moment many times over since his adolescence. The crowd of students in the auditorium waited patiently for him to start. They had come to hear his story and he had decided to tell it unadulterated.

"Thank you for this opportunity. I was born in this city and grew up here as well," he said and then smiled." "See the irony, someone who had never been past more than a year of college has been asked to deliver a speech to students who are about to complete their graduation. Nevertheless, I wanted to start my talk with a cautionary. You will hear my story today, but share it with caution with your parents when you go back home tonight."

The audience laughed, as he continued.

He checked with the audience if anyone remembered of a film that marked the debut of a popular Bollywood action hero that had the popular song, *Ek pal ka Jeena,* which translated in English would mean to live for a moment. The audience roared in acknowledgement. He then asked the audience, if they remembered the dance moves in the movie on that song. The audience echoed aloud in confirmation again.

"Do you remember the guy that was dancing, in the third row, fourth from the left as you saw the screen behind the hero?"

The audience responded in laughter negatively.

"That was me, the Superstar Struggler," he said as the audience broke into laughter.

"Don't laugh! That indeed was a big break for me back in the day. I had reached Mumbai from Kidderpore, two years before that day. I was a big star in my neighbourhood. No neighbourhood event would be complete without my show. The neighbours used to tell my father that he had named his son very aptly after the famous Bollywood hero Mithoon. He was quite proud of my talents perhaps more than what he should have been. He worked as a clerk in the Garden Reach area with the Port authorities. We were not poor, but comfortable because of the house that my father had inherited. The rental income from it was what made us comfortable. We were a family of four, me, my younger brother and my parents. Now back to the struggle. My father was very nervous when I told him that I want to go to Mumbai and struggle. He had struggled enough in his life and certainly did not want me to go through the same. He gave me two years and used to send me five thousand rupees every month. So this break was very timely as I could negotiate an extension with him for another two years. He agreed but nothing happened for me in those two years.

I gave my daily attendance at Prithvi Theatre in Mumbai, discussed dreams of stardom with other strugglers, who were also proudly known as actors. I sometimes even used to get scared to see some real super strugglers who had come to become hero in Bollywood, and were now making rounds to get roles of fathers and uncles that could even save the production house the cost of their makeup. I used to get scared thinking about them but there were also stories of success among strugglers. There were girls as well, who all aspired to be nothing less than Madhuri[39]." He paused to take a sip of water from the bottle that was kept on the lectern.

39 Famous Bollywood actress

"My father stopped sending me money and it had been three months that I had exhausted on my list of borrowers. There was no sign of luck or a role or a break. I was sharing a room with two other strugglers, who were getting bits and pieces of small roles and had advised me of the same. I had bluntly told them that I was not meant to do such insignificant roles, either stardom or nothing. This was a diplomatic blunder on my part since I was neither contributing for the rent nor food. They just could not take it on their ego and I was thrown out. I decided to go back to Kidderpore.

It was a couple of evenings later that Montu and I were standing at the tea stall at the corner of the busy street where the neighbourhood shops were lined up. The chill was in the air as winter was slowly setting in the city. The cool breeze from the river Hooghly added further to the chill. I saw from a distance a beautiful woman walking towards us. She seemed familiar, I thought while sipping the tea from the earthen cup. I recognized her as she come closer. I threw the earthen cup in the dustbin and was about to approach her, when I could feel some one holding me back. It was Montu.

I told him it's Mumtaaz. He replied that she is not alone. I looked at her again this time more carefully, how could I had missed observing the child in her arms. I could not resist and went ahead and greeted her. The child in her arms started crying just as I greeted her. She attempted to console the child and in an attempt to introduce the child to me, and asked the child to say hello to Mama[40].

Mama, I thought. I was speechless. I could have been something else if I had kept my promise to her and returned much earlier. Montu, few other friends and the banks of the river Hooghly were the witnesses of my undying love for Mumtaaz. I did not realise when I saw her after such a long time that Montu did tell me in an earlier phone conversation that Mumtaaz was getting married.

Montu looked at me with pity. Now guess what he asked me?

I had borrowed ten thousand rupees from Montu to go back to Mumbai, disregarding the threats from my father and overcoming all fears of struggle. I could not be anyone but an entertainer and I will be one, I had told myself, sitting by the window of the three tier compartment of the Mumbai bound train, as the cool night breeze hit my face. This time I had a determination that I could not explain anyone, even to myself, besides I had very little to lose from there.

It was couple of days after I went back to Mumbai when I met a fellow struggler, who advised me over a cutting chai[41] that with my tall frame, I should consider giving auditions for mythological daily soaps. He further mentioned that if I get the role, I would be wearing

40 Maternal Uncle in Bengali

41 tea

mythological costumes, with long beard and mustache, nobody would be able to recognize me. I could then continue my struggle for the movies in parallel. I liked the idea and for the next two weeks gave auditions for every mythological soap that was being aired or to be aired on television. So this was how I looked." He pressed the marker in his hand that got his photo in mythological attire on the screen behind him.

"It was the mythological soap called Goddess Manasa[42]," he continued, walking across the stage, "where I got my break. I played the character of Manasa's father, Sage Kashyapa. It was a break, synonymous to winning a jackpot in the world of strugglers. The end of that month I received a cheque of one hundred and fifty thousand rupees. It really made me scared of struggle. I had not ever earned that amount of money in my life. I comprised with my dreams. Mithoon Khan ensured that there would not be any other Mithoon in the industry who would need to become a Disco Dancer[43].

The pay cheque kept increasing every month and I began doing few more daily soaps. I became a successful mythological father, yet nobody recognized me when I was on the streets. I enjoyed the stability, there was no pleading to borrow money, no requesting the tea stall owner to have a cutting chai on credit. I had by then

42 Goddess of Snakes

43 Successful Bollywood movie where a renowned Bollywood actor acted

moved to a two-bed room apartment in Goregaon. My parents were finally happy. My brother, who had moved to USA as a software engineer, continued to laugh at me. I had paid back Montu's loan with my first pay cheque. I called him and asked him to join me in Mumbai. He is now my secretary. I felt comfortable and happy to have finally been able to relinquish my title of a struggler. I had achieved what I wanted, the new bunch of strugglers in Prithvi were now using me as the case study.

It was during these days, when the wife of the producer of one of my mythological soap was having a conversation with me over lunch in between shooting of a daily soap. She complained that the popular television channels were looking for a social drama, the era of mythological soap would soon be over. I felt the butterflies in my stomach. No way could I go back the days of my struggle from here on. She continued that she is looking for a story that had elements of struggle, romance, and finally personify success. I told her spontaneously without thinking much that I had a story that had all those elements that she was looking for. It was my story, the story of Superstar Struggler. That was how I became a successful writer. Superstar Struggler ran for four years and won me a lot of accolades. Mythological soaps slowly disappeared but that did not matter for me. I had by now become a successful writer. I have four dictaphones and four assistants.

Life sometimes is strange, as this moment could borrow its reality from you. Serendipity is often ignored. The things that I said many years back on the streets of Kidderpore were often dismissed and laughed at, but when I say those same things now keeping my feet on the boulders of Worli Seaface, they are considered as motivation. The world needs to recognize the Superstar in every Struggler.

Thank you."

He bowed finishing his speech as the audience broke into a loud applause for the Struggler who had now truly become a Superstar.

About The Author

Subhadip Mazumdar is an Indian Author born in Bihar, India. He grew up in Kolkata, where he completed his schooling from Don Bosco, Park Circus. He graduated in Electrical Engineering from Manipal Institute of Technology followed by his post graduation in Management Sciences from University of Canberra, Australia. He has been working in the Information Technology Industry for over two decades, both as an entrepreneur, and for large multi-national companies. His work had given him the opportunity to travel across multitude of countries covering both hemispheres. His travels motivated him to collect emotions, and thus present them through his first book Orange Sky and Blue Sun.

He can be reached at orangeskybluesun@gmail.com